MURDER! MYSTERY! MAYHEM!

Ten stories of nefarious crimes and detection

NORDIC PRESS

First Edition
Published
Nordic Press
Kindlyckevägen 13
Rimforsa, Sweden.
2022
This is a work of fiction. Similarities to real people, places, or events are entirely coincidental
Murder! Mystery! Mayhem!
978-91-987509-8-0
Cover Design by
David Green
llustrations by
Womba Dream
Formatted by
C. Marry Hultman
Edited by
Nordic Press

CASES

Ava

David Bowmore

Closing the office door and raising her lace veil, she turned to face me. I had to admit, she was a stunner. The sort of girl you always gave a second look.

Dark hair bounced around her shoulders under a small, tipped hat. Her big eyes were the colour of the Caribbean Sea. Dark red lips turned up in a shy smile. A knee length skirt showed off perfect calves. The jacket, when buttoned, accentuated her curves.

The scent of jasmine hit me like a wall.

'Are you Mr Carter?' she asked.

'That's what it says on the door.'

'Do you work with our kind?' Her eyes widened and then widened some more as they dilated. She was good.

'I work with the paying kind.'

'And how do you want paying, Mr Carter?' She rested her hand on her tilted hip, and one corner of her mouth raised seductively.

'Any respectable way that pays the rent.'

The smile dropped and she went over to the window. Not to look out through the blinds, she just went over to the window. I was getting the full three-sixty view. She turned back to me with a questioning look.

'You don't look like a private investigator.'

'That's probably a good thing, don't you think?'

She cocked her head to one side like a dog that recognises a favourite word.

'Oh yes, I see what you mean.'

'Please sit, Ms…'

'What do you want to call me?'

'By your name. You're my potential client, not the other way around.'

'Ava. My name is Ava,' she said as she sat on the wooden chair opposite my desk and crossed one leg over the other. They were legs worthy of a second, longer look.

'Do you have a last name?'

'Paige.'

'Well then, Miss Paige, what can I do for you?'

She opened her bag and pulled out a photograph. 'Two friends of mine have disappeared,' she said, placing the image on my desk.

'And your friends are like you?' I didn't pick up the picture, but lit a cigarette instead. It had been a long time coming but technological advances have now made the once dangerous habit safe, and it felt right to smoke in her presence.

'One of them is, yes.' She lifted the cigarette pack

from my desk. I hadn't offered, it's rude to offer. Ava took one out, tapped it on the pack.

'How long have they been missing?'

'Since this morning. We were due to go over some things.' The cigarette between her red lips impeded her speech as she lit it.

'You sure that's not just life getting in the way of your meeting. They could've been called away for any number of reasons.'

'The police didn't believe me either.'

'It's not that I don't believe you, miss, but it too soon.'

'I just know something has happened to them.' Her watery eyes pleaded for help, and I couldn't help feeling sorry for the girl.

'Were they mixed up in anything nefarious; drugs, weapons, prostitution?'

'No, definitely not.'

'If I were you, I'd keep trying to their numbers, call some friends and if I hadn't heard anything by this evening, then I'd call the police.'

'How many times, the police won't help. They never do with us even though we're citizens now.'

'The politics of the problem is not something I'll be able to fix. Where did you last see them?' I finally picked up the photo - handsome couple.

'At their home, yesterday.'

This surprised me. 'They own a house?'

'No. They worked at the university; a small room came with the job.'

I ignored the ire in her comment. Emotion wouldn't

get us anywhere.

'What did they do at the university?'

'She's a researcher and he lectures.'

'And how did you know them?'

She said with some pride, 'I'm a student of modern philosophy.'

This really did surprise me and my face couldn't help but show it.

'A girl can better herself, even a girl like me.'

'Sorry, but I thought you were a—'

'I can't help it. I'm programmed this way.'

Stunner or not, she was still an android. And I'd always preferred flesh and blood to plastic and metal; always have, always will.

▼▼▼

I'm old enough to remember when they first began to appear. Almost humans, from Korea and Japan. Designed to perform simple tasks like cleaning and security for the wealthy. I saw my first one at school when I was ten years old. He was used as a caretaker and security bot. A glossy white patrol man who swept the playground and emptied bins. He was programmed to recognise who was and wasn't meant to be there, and escort them off the premises if they weren't. Until he crushed the arm of an aunt who'd come to collect her sister's child.

Teething troubles – a glitch in the programme – a sign of things to come?

Newer, safer and more realistic models came out as more companies started to produce droids for all manner of tasks. Rolls Royce even produced them as chauffeurs and mechanics. Within twenty years, almost anyone could buy a fully compliant servant with complete working anatomy and an almost human voice box. As a younger man, I had friends who swore that pleasure droids were better than the real thing. You could do whatever you wanted with a pleasure droid, they never complained.

But it made me ever-so-slightly sick thinking about it.

▼▼▼

I've been on this planet for sixty years, so thoughts of her as anything other than a client should have been the furthest thing from my mind. But, as she said, she was programmed that way. To make people desire her.

'So, you're trying to deprogram.'

'Not exactly, more like expand my programming. I want to grow. I'm changing.'

'Can't you go to Android Health or a backstreet programmer for a quick fix?'

'Would you let someone mess with your brain? What if they get it wrong and wipe my personality? It does happen. The right programme in the right processing unit and a new or even pre-existing personality can be overlaid on the neural cortex, effectively deleting the first person.'

'So, you're doing it the old-fashioned way.'

She nodded her head. 'Through education.'

'But modern Philosophy – that's a bit of a jump

from your original programming.'

'Believe it or not, we have quite a lot of unused terabytes in our heads. We are more than capable of outgrowing our original programming.'

'So your friends, they're your what, tutors, professors?'

She nodded again, but her eyes never left mine. Where was the harm? If I could look into those blue pools a few more times, I'd take the case.

'Five hundred a day. How many days can you afford?'

'Two. Perhaps three if I go to work, but I'd rather not,' she said, blushing. Like I said, she was good.

'We'd better make a start then. Take me to their room and on the way, you can tell me everything you know about them.' I picked a raincoat off the hook by the door, and then held the door open for her. She passed through with a shy 'Thank you.' I'd never seen such a humanlike gesture from a droid, but then again, I didn't really know any. There was the cleaning droid that did every room in the block once a week, and some who worked with law enforcement, but I didn't mix with any socially.

▼▼▼

Ava sat in the passenger seat and her voice fell like cool river water over my old stony bones. It eased my mind and took me out of myself. I could almost have been young again. For the first time in a long time, I thought I was falling in—This was wrong. I had to concentrate on the story she told. Eyes on the road and not on her, definitely not on her.

Her friends were a mixed-race couple. Tom, human, mid-forties, and Miranda a mark-9v3, one of the last off the production line. Tom loved teaching and encouraging young minds, and Miranda had been a researcher since her activation in 2097. At first, she did lots of repetitive mundane tasks, filling tubes and recording data. She couldn't do anything else; her programming didn't allow it. But she did resent it, along with her lack of choices and freedom in her life.

They'd begun a relationship two years before the Android Bill of Rights was passed in Parliament, and until then had to see each other on the QT. Like every couple, they had their differences, but on the whole loved each other.

It was a concept I found difficult to accept. Surely, it's impossible for machinery to love. How could they feel that much joy and heartache? And yet, the very fact that androids gained rights and were no longer considered slave labour meant they, as a race, had passions. From the moment the emotion chips were invented they began to voice their concerns.

It is now illegal to create artificial sapient beings although no doubt some of the mega-wealthy would find some way around the restrictions. Androids live—if that's the word—longer than humans, but at least we can procreate. Ava sitting next to me, with her body that was too perfect, would never age and look the same for, perhaps, two or three hundred years. No one knows exactly how long. It depends on many factors. Parts will wear out and become difficult to replace. But one day she would cease to be able to function.

Droids caring for each other I could almost handle, but mixed relationships made me uncomfortable. I'm old-fashioned, I suppose. I lit another cigarette.

It wobbled between my lips as I asked, 'You don't mind, do you?'

'Why should I?'

The fabric of her skirt was pulled tight over her thigh. She saw me looking and I apologised. Her lips parted in a sad smile.

'What were they working on?' I asked turning my eyes away from her.

'Later. Turn left here.'

Students were protesting on the campus. An ever-changing rabble who thought they had invented placards and slogans, change and new ways of thinking; never fully appreciating the generations before who'd also fought for change. Their cries for equality often tended to undermine and belittle the achievements of the past. Student protestors: self-centred ideologists who, one day in the future, would become the bad guys in the eyes of eager youngsters.

Most of them were human. These days, androids can be difficult to tell apart from their human counterparts. However, they usually dress more conservatively, avoiding the counterculture look and opting for casual but comfortably sensible clothing, like Ava next to me. I reasoned that for Ava it was a chance to look respectable, rather than dress like a tart, which no doubt she'd had to do from the moment she first blinked.

‘What’s the protest for?’

‘Does it matter?’

She took me round the back of a large concrete building. In all the years of progress, why were institutions like this still big, grey, ugly slabs of concrete and glass? She waved her palm in front of a sensor by the door, which then clicked open. I followed as we climbed the stairs.

Before we entered, she said, ‘I came here this morning for a meeting, and they weren’t home. It worried me. They’re always where they’re meant to be. Always.’

She must have been one of their trusted students for she waved her palm in front of the viewer and the apartment door clicked open.

I hadn’t expected much, but the room was smaller than I imagined. Even with rights, androids would always be second rate citizens. Droidphobia made finding accommodation difficult and often limited their career options to jobs that came with rooms. Vagrant droids without a registered address were usually deactivated. And mixed couples were edged out of the mortgage market as a droid’s income was never taken into consideration. Rental was only an option if an understanding landlord could be found. These two were lucky to work together in a well-respected and liberal university. I wonder what sort of rooms a human couple would have.

This room was small with a kitchenette on the far wall, which housed a window overlooking the car park. A two-seater sofa sat under a vid-link screen on the wall opposite the bed. It displayed art in a slow loop. Two small desks faced the remaining wall: both cluttered with paperwork, pens and screens. Presumably, the only other door in the room led to the bathroom or more likely the shower room. But what really caught my eye were the two corpses on the bed.

I watched Ava as she looked from me to the bodies and then back again.

'But—' she began.

'Where do you suppose they come from?' I said, going over to check their status. It was clear the man was dead. A large knife protruded from his chest. Blood soaked the sheets, spilling over the edge onto the floor where it still dripped like an old faucet – plip… plip.

It's more difficult to tell if an Android has been deactivated. But she was unresponsive to my attempts to rouse her. The black scorch marks around the charging port behind her right ear didn't bode well. It looked like her cortex had been fried. If that were the case, there'd be very little chance of getting any data from her CPU.

'And you're sure they weren't here earlier?'

'Of course I am!' Water welled in her eyes. I'd never seen an android cry before. I wanted to hold her in my arms and tell her it would be okay. God, did she have to give off so much pheromone?

'You'd better tell me what they were working on.'

She sat at the little table, and after a few seconds pause said, 'Fusion.'

'Fusion? Fusion of what?'

'Of android and biological bodies. To be specific, the birthing of a human incubated in an android body. A walking artificial womb.'

'Are you serious?'

‘Yes.’ She wiped her eyes with a handkerchief pulled from her handbag.

‘Surely, that’s impossible?’

‘Everything was impossible once. Tell a person from the dark ages that one day we would fly through the air travelling thousands of miles and they’d have called it witchcraft, or tell Queen Victoria about electric light, or telephones, or screens that report images of events from across the globe the instant they happen, and she’d have declared you mad and probably sent you to Bedlam. With Science, anything is possible—anything. Look at me or any droid for that matter; exact working replicas of human beings with emotional needs, a willingness to strive and be a part of the community. A hundred years ago androids were fictions in books and on screens, now we walk amongst you, work with you, sleep with you. So why shouldn’t it be possible? We know we can’t live forever and will eventually stop functioning. And that’s because governments are afraid of us, or the potential superiority of metal over meat. Doesn’t it make sense to want to survive, to leave something behind, as humans do? It may well be the next evolutionary steps, Mr Carter.’

‘But… it’s disgusting…’

For the first time she gave me the sort of look you get when you’ve let someone down; the sort of look that told me I wasn’t the man she thought I might be.

‘Let’s go outside?’ she said.

‘Sure.’ So we did.

‘May I have one of those?’ she asked as I lit a cigarette.

I handed her the pack. What is it about a woman smoking that is so attractive? Is it that bad woman vibe or something more… sexual? I had to stop seeing her this way. She was just a machine. I'd never been with a droid in my life, and I didn't intend to start with Ava.

'What made you so special?'

'I was helping them on the project. I'm not on the staff or anything, but I've a yearning. Miranda called me broody. So I agreed to be a mother should they get anywhere in their research. And they were getting very close. I was due to have an artificial womb of my own.'

I was stunned. How could such a thing be possible? Where could it all end?

▼▼▼

Detectives soon arrived, along with scene of crime units, community officers, campus security, an ambulance crew and an android investigation team—code breakers at the ready. Code breakers - like a mash-up of old truncheons and tazers send a large current of electricity through a droid just by touching the baton to their skin, deactivating it for several hours.

Ava and I sat outside on the steps of the building while the Busys got busy inside. Detective Cole was known to me. I can't say I ever liked the man, but he was always professional. Almost too professional.

'I told you, Cole. She came to me for help.'

'Let her answer the questions, Carter.'

I gave her the nod and told her it would be okay.

'I don't want you sticking your nose in, Carter,'

Cole said, after Ava had made her statement.

'Will you at least let me know if you find any information as to who the killer is?' I felt I had to try to help Ava. But I couldn't express why.

Cole put it more succinctly. 'You were commissioned to find two missing people. You found them. Case closed.'

'Be reasonable, Cole.'

'Forget it and go home. Drink, smoke, watch sport. Do whatever it is you do, but don't get involved in this.'

He turned from me. 'Miss Paige, don't leave town, but do leave your contact details with my colleague, and be sure to give him your serial number too.'

'I don't have to do that,' she said.

'If I take you to the station, you won't be given a choice.'

The threat hung in the air like a bad smell. Androids were usually powered down in the cells. Androids had rights, but not human rights.

She went to the colleague and a few minutes later returned to me.

'Would you take me home, Mr Carter?'

I pulled the car out and made my way past the protesters again. One of them jumped on the bonnet and licked the windscreen. Ava looked away, staring through the door window. The protester jumped off the car with a rebel yell. Things would soon turn nasty. I could see the black mask brigade gather on the fringes of the crowd.

'Idiots,' I said.

She continued to look at the buildings as they whooshed by.

'I'm sorry about what I said back there.'

'It doesn't matter.' She didn't move.

'Where do you live?'

'There's a place in town. There's a room I can recharge in when I'm not working.'

'You mean—'

'Exactly.'

She'd had so much taken away from her. Her friends and educators. A chance at motherhood and perhaps a new way of living. A future that was opening for her had had the door firmly closed in her face. I couldn't let her go back to her old work; not until she had a chance to assimilate it all. 'Come to my place,' I said, knowing I would regret the offer.

'Why?'

'So you don't have to work.' I added, 'I have a spare room. You can have it for the night, or until you feel better.'

She acquiesced with a shrug of her shoulders. I must have been mad.

The cat hissed and ran out though the open door, keen to be on the prowl. I smiled and almost apologised before bolting the door.

'Go on through to the living room. Do you want anything?'

'What do you mean?'

'To eat or drink?'

'I don't need anything.'

I rehydrated a coffee—best ten-second espresso in the apartment—before going through to the living room. She sat on the sofa flicking through the screen looking for news.

'Who could have done it?' she asked.

'Someone who objected to their research would be the obvious guess.' I lit another cigarette.

'But they were so careful. Only I knew about it.' She held out a hand indicating that she wanted a smoke. I passed her the pack.

'Do you really get something from these things.'

'What do you mean?'

'Do they relax you or is it just … I don't know… habit?'

'I'm a pleasure droid, Mr Carter. I like pleasure. My programming reacts to all forms of pleasurable stimuli. It makes me better at giving pleasure in return.' She held up the now lit cigarette. 'These are easy pleasure.'

'Sorry.'

'What for? You didn't program me.' She blew a smoke ring towards me, but her eyes held no warmth.

After a few minutes of silence, she said, 'Do you suppose the government could have had anything to do with it?'

'What?'

'Government agents. Tom was paranoid about anyone finding out about the project. The law is quite rigid about manufacturing androids. We knew that impregnating a droid would be called manufacturing. He had us worried.'

'He sounds like a randy bugger, with a God complex, who wanted to have his way with two female droids.'

'That's disgusting. He was a great man trying to do what was right. Anyway, In Vitro Fertilization is the only way to move forward. It will be a long time before a more natural pregnancy can occur. And then, human DNA can start to improve.'

We sat in silence. I tried not to look at her fingers as they toyed with the cigarette, or how her lips clasped the filter as she inhaled the smoke.

'Don't you need a human egg? Where was that coming from?'

'I didn't know about that. I just wanted to be the mother. But that's not going to happen now, is it?

'I still owe you for a half a day's work.' She opened her bag, but I waved her gesture away.

'I didn't do anything. Your room's over there. I'm in here.' I stood and pointed at the door behind me and the one opposite. 'Do you need to recharge?'

'I'm good.' She kicked off her mules. Her toenails were princess pink. Such a little girl colour.

In my room, there's an old oak desk. A hand me down from my grandfather, inlaid with green leather, a reminder of a more elegant time. I sat at it, trying to focus on the Anderson case notes.

The Anderson case; a simple tailing job. I'd followed Cassie Anderson every day for a month at the request of her successful, but cantankerous, husband. As soon as he had evidence of her betrayal, he'd start divorce proceedings. And she'd be left with nothing.

Looking at her photograph I was once again struck by a deep sense of strength. But for all my following, I hadn't seen anything out of the ordinary. She shopped with friends, met her sister, volunteered in a charity shop, raised money for orphans, and went to church services. As far as I could tell she was a kind, religious and particularly good woman.

I'd have to tell Mr Anderson that he was wasting his money employing me. I poured a whisky. It would have been easy to string him along, but I wasn't that sort of private detective.

The news channel theme tune floated to me from the living room.

The sooner this droid was out of my life, the better.

I wasn't falling in love.

I pulled up Mr Anderson's email. Sent the template notifying him that nothing of an unusual, illegal or upsetting nature occurred in the three weeks I had been in his employ, with copies of all the photos, and a final bill payable within thirty days.

And then I nearly spilt my coffee. One of the images flashed across my memory. How had I not seen it for what it was earlier? I suppose I was too distracted by the dead human to worry about the defunct droid. I opened the gallery again. Yes. In one photo she, Miranda mark-9v3, was at the table next to Mrs Anderson and her friends. My notes on that day told me she had come and gone on her own. It was, as far as I knew, the only time Miranda had come into close contact with Mrs Anderson. My recording of the conversation gave nothing away as to why Miranda was there.

I would need to speak to Mrs Anderson. Tricky if I wasn't to give my client away. And then I had a Eureka moment. Ava. Ava could talk to her. If we hurried, Mrs Anderson would still be at her charity work.

Ava agreed to help without batting an eyelid.

So, Ava went to find Mrs Anderson, and I called on her husband. He was a director of an insurance broker, with a flash office in the city. I was kept waiting for an hour until he finally allowed me access via the droid on reception. His desk was large and very old, like something out of a gothic castle. It put my little one to shame, but mine had sentimental value. And I'm sure nothing ever got to Mr Anderson's sentimental side. I wasn't invited to sit. Fine by me, I'd been there long enough anyway.

'I thought we were done, Mr Carter. My secretary will arrange payment.'

'Thank you, but I'm here on a separate matter.'

'How intriguing, or perhaps the word is coincidental. Continue.' He sat back in the chair, folded his hands under his chin. I expected him to call me Mr Bond and start stroking a white cat.

'In the course of my tracking, I came across a droid called Miranda who is linked to another case I'm working on. I wondered if you knew her.'

'It. I refuse to think of these things as anything other than machines.'

'You employ at least one,' I said referring to the receptionist.

'Cheap labour, Mr Carter. That is all.'

'But did you know her.' I passed my pad over with a cropped image of Miranda on it.

'No.' He barely glanced at it.

'Look again, please.'

With a sigh, he did as I asked and said, 'No. Never seen it before.'

'Thank you, Mr Anderson.'

I met Ava back at my flat. She'd had a shower and wore one of my robes. That scent hung around her again—jasmine.

'How did it go?' I asked.

'Not well.'

'Never mind. Do you have a recording or memory that can be downloaded? It might be easier than a report.'

'My memories are protected by my rights and can only be accessed with a warrant from a judge, Mr Carter.'

'Sorry. I only meant—'

'But I suppose I could let you have a peek.' She gave me that sad smile again and added, 'VR unit, please.'

I dug around in a box under the sink and passed her an old cable. She put one end behind her neck, under her hairline—presumably under a special flap or cover—and the other end into a VR helmet by the entertainment unit. I placed it on my head. A gentle buzz indicated a deep connection with my brain's own electrical impulses, which bound my senses to the machine allowing me to share Ava's memories.

Everything darkened as the vizor lowered. Numbers and letters flashed faster than I could read. I thought I saw a date before total darkness took hold.

An image of a busy high street with shoppers meandering and cars travelling emerged from the emptiness. We're scanning to the left looking up the street and then to the right. The motion is quick and makes me nauseous. We cross the street focusing on the shop. For a moment we look at a child in a pram as the mother pushes past.

Then we look at the rail of second-hand clothes outside the shop. Now we're pushing the door open and striding toward the counter where Mrs Anderson serves an old lady. We're looking at the old lady, the grey hair in particular fascinates me. She says something about her grandson. She goes away and I turn towards Mrs Anderson, who looks at me with a work smile that doesn't reach her eyes. I've smiled those smiles before.

At that moment, I wasn't sure who I was; me, her or us.

'We need to talk about Tom and Miranda.' Ava's voice is strange in my head.

Mrs Anderson opens her mouth like a letter 'o' but no sounds comes out, and she looks at the image on my pad. Then she parts hanging beads in the door to the staff area. 'Back in five,' she calls to her colleague who then steps out and looks at me disapprovingly. She is old and hard around the edges. Mrs Anderson leads the way outside and now we're walking along the pavement.

'How did you know?'

'Your reaction.' It's Ava's voice but sounds like me in my head.

'I knew he had someone special, but—'

'Yes, he did.'

'Oh. He said it wasn't serious, just complicated and that…'

Then Mrs Anderson pauses and looks at us with a confused look on her face.

'What do you mean 'did'?'

'Tom died this morning. He was killed.' And my vision is blurring now. My hands wipe tears away but they won't stop coming.

A scream hurts my ears and I focus on Mrs Anderson who is trying to gulp air. We try to hold her as she stumbles backwards and crumples to the ground. She sobs into my shoulder. I can smell apples in her hair. A small crowd has gathered and want to know what I've done to upset her.

'It's a droid. Stop it before it kills her.'

'No. I'm trying to help,' I plead.

'Fucking bots are always fucking with us, taking our fucking jobs.' Someone out of the crowd grabs my hair. I feel a kick to her stomach, another to her back. Mrs Anderson is still crying. As I'm dragged away, I see the old woman comforting her. I stumble as we break free of the man dragging me by the hair. My vision is all over the place. I'm looking at Ava's feet as they try to keep me upright. I'm glancing over my shoulder as I stagger away. We run into a streetlamp, but I don't feel the pain.

I pulled the VR unit from my head to find myself on my knees. I couldn't bear the shame she felt. I couldn't bare my guilt. Do we really hate droids so much?

'I'm sorry,' I said.

'It's not your fault.' She put her arms around me. I held her tight, and it felt right.

'I should never have asked for your help.'

I pulled back from her. She un-jacked the cable and settled her hair in place.

'You okay?' I ask.

'I feel better now I'm here,' she said, as I looked into watery eyes.

'Stop it, Ava. Don't come any closer, please.'

But she did. Her lips were soft and warm.

I couldn't let this happen. It wasn't natural. Not for me at any rate. So I pushed her away. Told her it was for the best, that I was going to bed, we'd talk more in the morning, and I turned away from those lovely pleading Caribbean blue eyes.

I woke, surprised that I had slept at all, with Ava still on my mind. It had taken a tremendous amount of will power to push her away when I wanted her warmth so much. A small part of me, at the back of my head, wanted to embrace this idea of her companionship. While another larger part reminded me that it wasn't real, her flesh was grown in a tank to cover plastic and metal moving parts, nothing more. That her heart is only a battery and her brain only a wet bio-comp. The small part of me replies that all brains are bio computers, and a heart is only a muscle that keeps us going, not really all that different from a rechargeable battery, except we charge ours with calories.

I pushed these biological arguments aside and sat up.

I'd go across to her room and see how she was. Maybe tell her I needed more time to come to terms with things. I didn't want to hurt her feelings, but I wanted to help. And there I was again questioning what goes on in an android's mind, when I'd seen it with my own senses. The fear she'd felt, the shame as she ran away from the mob who thought she was attacking a human.

But I wanted to be with her so much. I didn't want her to work the way she was programmed. After all, she was trying to grow, and her hopes had been dashed. I thought that maybe I could give her work. Perhaps, train her up, help her reprogram herself with new skills. She could be my assistant. I had two rooms, so she could live with me, and she didn't need to eat, therefore the outgoings on the apartment wouldn't be increased. I'd pay her, and who knew perhaps one day I could make her a partner. Someone to run the agency after I'd gone. And surely that would be a better relationship than any romantic one, wouldn't it?

I showered, dressed, made coffee. When she didn't come out of her room, I tapped on the door. No answer. I tried the handle. The door swung inwards, and I crumpled to my knees.

'No, no, no, no, noooo!'

Ava lay sprawled backwards over the bed, fully clothed and clearly deactivated. The light of life—yes life—had gone from her eyes. I crawled forward and moved the hair aside so I could see her charging port. The flesh was blackened and burnt, and her hair was badly singed. Like Miranda, she'd had her cortex fried.

My chance of some sort of happiness stolen before I could figure out if I even wanted it.

I don't know how long I sat with her, but eventually I moved my numb limbs and went to make the call.

When androids gained their rights, it became law to report the 'death' of one. Before that if a droid was deactivated it was sent to the recyclers or dumped in the back yard or a shed at the bottom of the garden. Some were sold to farmers as scarecrows. An owner of a droid could deactivate it for any number of reasons, but since they were now classed as people their death had to be reported.

I called detective Cole direct. The two cases had to be linked.

'What makes you say that?' Cole asked as he looked down at Ava.

'Even you can see it, can't you? They knew each other and they were killed the same way.'

'But Miranda's partner was also killed, and contrary to popular belief you're alive and kicking.'

'I'm not her partner. There was nothing between us. It must have something to do with the murderer.'

'But that could be you, couldn't it?'

'Oh come off it, Cole. You can't be serious?'

'Oh I am very serious.'

'But I lo…I mean she meant… I didn't want to see her hurt. I didn't want her working the way she did. I was just trying to help her.'

He laughed then. A small condescending smirk of pity.

'You should be questioning a Mr Anderson.'

'Why?'

'His wife was having a thing with Tom.'

'And how do you know this? Why didn't you say anything yesterday?'

'Only found out yesterday. I talked to him while Ava went to see Cassie Anderson. The woman fell apart in the street when Ava told her about Tom. Mr Anderson said he didn't know him. He's lying of course.'

'Might not be.'

'He wanted me to follow her. He suspected her of something. My guess is he found out from some other source about their affair and had him killed.'

'And why kill the droid?'

'I don't know. He doesn't like them, that's for sure.'

He turned to the android tech and asked, 'Anything?'

'Deep fried chips.'

When I gave a questioning look, she said, 'She's had a hundred thousand watts pushed through her electronics.'

The scent of melted plastic and pork crackling filled the room.

'Okay. Don't go anywhere, Carter. We'll send someone up from disposal.'

I sat on the edge of the bed, reached out a hand and pushed the hair back from her face.

▼▼▼

The weeks passed.

As Ava said, the police weren't interested in the deactivation of androids. Detective Cole questioned Mr and Mrs Anderson but found no evidence of an affair. Mrs A had time to compose herself and denied any suggestion of an affair between her and Tom. The case is still open, but not active.

And that was that, or so it seemed.

A year later I had to travel north to be with my mother who'd taken a turn for the worse and was now in hospital. A stomach thing brought on by years of eating yeasty, sugar-filled vegan food, for breakfast, lunch, and dinner.

The weeks of her death stretched. Everyone knew

the end was coming, but no one could do anything to ease her pain. Modern science – what a joke? We can create living machines, but we can't stop people dying.

I was sitting with my mother one evening, flicking through an old magazine, trying to ignore the occasional groans that escaped her drug-induced sleep, when a voice said, 'Mr Carter?'

I looked up and saw a plump, middle-aged nurse with dark brown hair and caring eyes. Not a woman, a droid. An early model designed for utility work, to sink invisibly into the background, while they carried out basic household tasks like cleaning or gardening. Her name tag said Sarah Elmhurst.

'Yes?'

'Nothing.'

I went back to the magazine while she checked the chart and made sure my mother was comfortable. But I could see her mind was not completely on the task in hand. She kept looking at me when she thought I wouldn't notice.

'How is she?' I asked.

She tilted her head to one side. 'As expected.' It's the usual reply when there's no hope.

Something about her reminded me of the cleaner at my apartment block. But these models all had a similar look.

When my stint with Mother was over, I kissed my sister on the cheek and told her to phone if there was any change. We both knew what I meant; the end was coming.

In my car, I pulled the data pad out of the glove

compartment and logged into the electoral register. Whether android or human, the councils had to know the stats for voting purposes. Androids aren't eligible to vote—not yet—but their accommodation address had to on the register.

I knocked at the black door of a small, terraced house. A baby wailed inside. The nurse answered.

'Ava?'

For a few seconds she looked lost, but then opened the door wider, stepped back and said, 'You'd better come in.'

She led me through to a small sitting room with an even smaller kitchen off it. A crib in the corner housed the crying child. I went over, tickled its chin.

'Nice place you got here. Good landlord?'

'Yes, and sympathetic.'

'I'm glad. Should I call you Miranda?'

She reached for a pack of cigarettes, and said, 'How did you know?'

'It didn't take long after you died for me to come to my senses. It was only after I was clear of you that I started to think rationally, and a few things you said came back to me. For instance, you used the past tense several times before we found the bodies. And then there was the long speech about equality and progress. Very impassioned, but hardly the sort of thing a droid programmed as Ava was would have come out with. And when I thought about it, it was you who told me how easily an android personality could be overwritten.'

She lit a cigarette, blew a smoke ring with perfectly pouted lips, and for a few seconds everything about this her was all Ava.

'Who are you really? Does it go further back than Miranda?'

'No, I'm Miranda,' she said.

'Why did you visit Cassie Anderson?'

'Curiosity. I'd suspected and wanted to know what her appeal was. Once I'd met her, I rationalised that it wouldn't last, there was nothing to the woman, but a few days later he told me he wanted to leave. He was tired of fighting, of the prejudice, and all the hostility. He was just going to turn his back on all we'd fought for and everything we wanted to achieve. Something snapped. I lashed out. I shouldn't have been able to harm him, not permanently. The knife killed him almost instantly.

'Seconds later, Ava arrived for her tutorial and let herself in. I overpowered her with a code breaker.'

'It's illegal to own one of those.'

'And yet the police can use them with impunity. How is that fair?'

'Life has never been fair.'

'It's less fair for us.' She took a slow breath. 'I placed a VR over her head, plugged in, broke the default passwords and deleted Ava. Then I mirrored myself into a blank neural cortex. She couldn't put up any resistance. It took a few hours, but when I woke in my new body, the old Ava was gone – well, most of her. A few mannerisms remained, some programming essentials, but nothing of her personality.

'My old body lay slumped, empty of a soul you might say. So I dragged it to the bed and overloaded the cortex with the same code breaker, simply plugged it directly into the access point and left it on till everything was fried. Disturbing to watch but terribly easy.'

'Why come to my office?'

'I needed an alibi. You were the nearest semi-professional I could find. Fortunately, Ava's body was equipped to flummox you. You wanted to protect her, even desired her. Male meat is so easy to manipulate.'

Cold vitriol dripped from her words.

'I mean, you didn't need an alibi. You should have just left the bodies. They'd have been found and you—the murderer—would be in a new body anyway.'

'I realise that now, but I wasn't thinking clearly.'

'And then, while I slept, you killed again. Where did you find this body?'

'She was an old cleaner unit in your block, emptying bins, making sure dust didn't build up in the corners, mopping the stairs. I stayed for a few weeks so as not to raise suspicion.'

'Who notices the cleaner?'

'How arrogant meat is.' More venom.

My phone rang.

'Do you like working at the hospital?' I asked, ignoring my sister's call.

'It's better than anything Ava ever did.'

'What about the project?'

'That can wait. I'm on an extended sabbatical. Somehow, I'm not quite the same person I once was. Something of Ava and a bit of Sarah have softened me.'

'And this child,' I picked the baby up, rocked it in my arms, 'Whose is it?'

'She's a neighbour's. If I can, I help out while she's

at work.' Her eyes started to fill with water.

'Still dreaming of being a mother?'

Before she could answer, someone knocked on the front door. Automatically, she went to answer it. Cole's squad quickly zapped her with a code breaker. It was over before it had begun.

My sister rang again. I was needed at the hospital.

Cole thanked me for the tip off and told me to come to the local station when I was ready. By then, they would have downloaded everything they needed from Miranda and scraped the unit. And my Ava would be gone forever.

The electric engine ticked over with a gentle hum as I pressed the starter button.

On a street corner stood a woman; badly dressed, dragging deeply on a cigarette for warmth, hoping for a client. I drove on leaving her to the mercy of the cold and the night.

A message from my sister scrolled across my watch. HURRY.

I sighed; it was going to be a long night.

DAVID BOWMORE

David was born in a gypsy caravan, on a wintery night with the sound of thunder and the flash of lightning welcoming him into the world.

Forty-five years later, he started writing fiction.

He has lived here, there and everywhere. For the time being, he lives in Yorkshire with his wonderful wife and a small white poodle.

In his time, he has worn many hats; chef, teacher and landscape gardener.

His award-winning book of connected short stories 'The Magic of Deben Market' was performed by BookStreamz in December 2020, starring Leslie Ash, Kelli Hollis, and John Hales as Moony Moore.

Discover more about David's writing at www.davidbowmore.co.uk

What You Should Have Done

Margaret Karmazin

Vanessa Nielsen awoke after her husband was already out of bed, then remembered he had flown to Portland the night before on a consulting job. He traveled too damn much, but it all came with an excellent salary; she could not complain about *that*. They had decided when Caden was born that she would quit her job as a speech therapist and devote all of her attention to their son.

When she entered Caden's bedroom to wake him for school, the shock of seeing the boy's empty bed caused her to feel that her heart would explode. She rushed about calling his name. He was not in the closet, nor under the bed, not in other bedrooms or bathrooms, not anywhere. Panicked, she ran downstairs and through the rooms, yelling his name. Caleb was nowhere.

Officer Linda Styles reported all of this to Lieutenant Char Perez and Sergeant Maurice Booker, who had just arrived at the scene. "She's almost hysterical," Styles said as she finished.

"Well, I guess *so*," said Char. "Has anyone called about ransom?"

"No," said Styles.

Char and Booker climbed the front steps into the impressive home set back from the street. The Nielsens lived in the high end of Montbleu where the houses were mostly all white with black shutters and the size of small mansions. "How many rooms do you think are in this place?" Char muttered to her sergeant.

"Ten or eleven?" he said. As usual, he was dressed immaculately in a custom-tailored suit, this time gray with a lighter gray shirt and dusky rose tie. He was six feet three inches tall and the color of Lindt dark chocolate, something Char would know since she was addicted to the stuff. He wore a one caret diamond in his left ear that he said he had had made from his aunt's former engagement ring after she died in the World Trade Center on 911.

They met the distraught mother inside the vestibule, decorated with a dark red Persian rug and ultramodern chandelier. "My, my," muttered Char under her breath.

Officer Styles handed Vanessa Nielsen over to her superiors and went to join another officer who was giving the house and yard another go-over. Missing kids often hid nearby.

Vanessa motioned for Char and Booker to sit down, which they did on the soft leather sofa adorned with posh fringed throw pillows. A large, tiled fireplace was the centerpiece of one wall with floor to ceiling bookshelves each side. "Tell us what happened," opened Char and Vanessa, holding a wadded tissue, did. "My husband is flying home tonight," she finished up.

"Were any of the doors or windows open when you came downstairs?" asked Char.

Vanessa shook her head. "I checked for that, no. They were all closed and locked."

"Do you have a basement?"

"Yes, but the officers checked down there. We have one of those steel basement doors with steps going down in, but they were closed and locked."

"Is there a way into the second floor from outside?" asked Booker with his pad open and pen poised. He liked to take notes the old-fashioned way.

She shook her head and began to cry again.

"How old is your son?" asked Char.

"Six," his mother said. "He's in first grade at Bayward."

"Bayward?" said Char.

"It's a private, very progressive school in Clarks Summit. He is picked up every morning. They respect our views on things and fortunately, we can afford to send him there."

Char caught an upper-class inflection to the woman's tone and felt it was not natural but cultivated.

"Your views?" she said.

"On health, diet and general education," Vanessa replied. "We are lacto-ovo vegetarians, for example, and they respect that."

"Anything else?" said Booker.

She shook her head impatiently. “I don’t see what this has to do with my missing child. I sincerely doubt that anyone at Bayward kidnapped him.”

“You never know,” said Char. “We like to cover all bases. We’ll contact the school if necessary. Who comes into this house besides you and your husband?”

She looked nonplussed. “Well, several people! We have guests, of course - friends, Jared’s work associates. My mother, his parents and our cleaner, Carla. She’s here once a week, sometimes more if we need her.”

“We’ll need a list of those names,” said Booker. “With contact numbers.”

Char stood up. “And who has a key to the house.”

“Wait,” said Vanessa, also standing up. “I forgot about Jared’s sister Lindsay.”

“Oh?”

“I don’t mean she has a key to the house. We would never give her a key to the house! She is certifiable and I mean that literally. Untreated whatever; they’ve never given her a firm diagnosis. Maybe a mix of bipolar and schizo, I don’t know, but half the time she refuses to take her meds. She’s a drain on the family, has driven Jared’s parent to consider moving to some undisclosed location, but every time they decide to stick it out and hope for the best. None of us except Jared give her our cell numbers; otherwise, we’d never have a moment’s peace.”

Vanessa rose from her perch on the edge of her loveseat, smoothed her tan wool slacks and said, “I’ll give you her address. She never answers her phone.” Her expression was one of disgust. “She has been, I’ll tell you, a large stress on our marriage. Jared has a soft spot for her." Her mouth pursed.

"Does Carla, your cleaner, have a key to the house?" Booker asked.

Vanessa was standing now, making an elegant figure despite her distress. She had resumed gently weeping and pulled a tissue from a hidden box on a sleek cherry end table. "No," she said. "I'm usually always here when she arrives and if not, she uses the key to the back door from a hidden spot out back."

"Why didn't you mention that earlier?" said Char, trying not to appear annoyed. "Show us."

They followed Vanessa through the smartly furnished house and out onto a large and colorfully furnished deck. Between some potted plants, she pulled down what appeared to be an electric socket and there, stuck magnetically to a metal plate was the key.

"Ah," said Booker, bending down to look at it. "Clever." Char could hear his brain clicking as he planned to install one on his own house. He stood back up.

"So, the key is there," Char said. "Try it to make sure it hasn't been replaced."

Vanessa did and it worked.

"It would appear then that whoever took Caden either had their own key to the house somehow or knew about this one." She was, meantime, wondering if all was well between Vanessa and her husband, considering her description of the troublesome sister.

"You and your husband- "Char began, but the woman had read her mind.

"We're fine," Vanessa said. "We have a very happy marriage, aside from the Lindsay thing."

“We’ll need photos of your son,” said Char. “And the team is ready to go over his room and the house. Please do not move or touch anything.”

Vanessa scrolled through photos on her phone and emailed several to Char’s.

Booker signaled to the CSI crew who had been quietly waiting in the vestibule.

Once in the car, Char said to Booker, “Let’s get the supposedly crazy sister-in-law over with first.”

He started the engine.

Char, who was short and compact with practically uncontrollable and sometimes frizzy black hair, removed the elastic she used to pull it all back, combed it with her fingers and once again made a ponytail.

“Nice to have so much hair,” said Booker, who often did his best to help his boss feel better about herself. In spite of her empathy for distraught victims of crime, Char’s lack of confidence about her persona managed to creep in after contact with a sleek, fashionable female like Vanessa.

“Hmmmph,” she said.

“I know what you’re thinking,” he said, “and I don’t know why you do it.”

The two of them had this conversation or one similar relatively frequently. They had worked together for three years and knew each other, or at least what each one allowed the other to see, quite well.

She had been comparing herself to the distressed mother with her elegant look and clothing, something Char always did when presented with chic women. Her own attractiveness, and she was in fact nice-looking in a haphazard way, had never been apparent to her. Booker, handsome as all get out, though technically happily married, being the good friend he was, never failed to reassure her. She was bisexual, which should work to her advantage in a potentially wider selection of sexual partners, yet she spent most of her time single and alone. She made little attempt to find someone and sometimes wondered if the problem was her partner who took up most of the space in her mind not devoted to working on cases. He was for all practical purposes, besides her psychologist sister Corina, her only close friend. Only he and Corina knew about her failed love affairs and her frequently broken heart. She had a penchant for unsuitable romantic partners.

"I don't know either," she said.

He went further than he ever had before and said, "If I were single and you weren't my boss, I'd think you were way more appealing than that supposedly high-class type back there."

Char felt thrilled though she knew she totally should not and could not ever admit it, so she just grunted in reply, albeit gratefully. "Life is lonely," she finally allowed herself to remark.

"Yes, it is," Booker replied, and she did not dare ask a man who was supposedly happily married what he meant by that.

Char looked at the photos of the little boy. "He's cute as a button," she said. The child was brown haired with a sweet, round face and large dark eyes. "He doesn't look like his mother."

Lindsey Nielson lived in a walk-up apartment over

a gift shop and florist. Hers was one of two apartments upstairs, though the other was empty, door currently wide open. She was napping when they arrived and not too pleased by the interruption.

Flashing their badges, Char glanced around, looking for signs of a kid, and said, “Where were you between the hours of, say, eight last evening and eight this morning?”

“Huh?” said Lindsey, rubbing her eyes. Her hair looked like she had combed it with an eggbeater. “What the hell? I was here, why? I took my freakin’ meds and slept for a goddamn age! And I still feel like shit warmed over.” She picked up a pack of Marlboros, shot one out violently and lit it. “What do you want?”

Booker said, “Do you mind if I look around?”

She shrugged and waved her hand at the place. Booker disappeared into the hallway.

“Your nephew, Caden Nielsen, disappeared during the night. Apparently, he’s been kidnapped.”

“No shit,” said Lindsay. “That’s not good.” She paused, then said. “Cute kid, stuff shirt parents. My brother, the great upper crust know-it-all, and that holier-than-thou bitch he married. A real fun pair.”

Char glanced around at the general disarray, though in spite of what Vanessa had said about her sister-in-law, she was not picking up dangerous vibes from her. Dangerous vibes actually often came from the most self-controlled people.

Booker reappeared, having completed his search, and gave Char a subtle all-clear sign.

“You wanna sit down?” said Lindsay. “Something

to drink? I don't get much company, but I do have beer in the fridge."

Now in her early forties, she had probably been pretty once, with her shaggy brown hair and large gray eyes. But now her skin was blotchy, and her face bloated, her fingernails dirty and a scabbed scratch ran along her cheek. Had she done that to herself? Having dealt with depression once herself, Char was sympathetic to those who suffered from mental illness but not so much when they refused to stay on their meds.

"Do you know anyone who'd want to kidnap the kid?" Booker asked. "Anyone who exhibited odd behavior around him?"

She shrugged. "I'm hardly ever around him," she said. "They don't want me over there. I spill things, haha. The last time was maybe six months ago, my father's birthday or something. It was just the family. Well, and their cleaner, Carla. She's okay. Though I think she steals their booze." She giggled.

"Any weird neighbors?"

Lindsay laughed. "They don't socialize with the neighbors, not unless somebody new moved in. You know, people who are on their level of society?" She snorted.

"We were told that you suffer from emotional or mental illness?" said Char. "Could you elaborate on that?"

"Screw them!" Lindsay shouted. "Like they know anything about my life! They know *nothing!* I have a few problems, sure, but I see somebody, okay? I have it under control. You know, not everybody is born with everything going their way!"

Char backed up slightly and Booker stood beside her. "It's okay, Lindsay," he said. "You've been helpful." He handed her his card. "If you think of anything that could help us further, don't hesitate to call."

She calmed down and managed to give him a come-hither look, which was ludicrous considering her general appearance and demeanor.

"Thank you, Lindsay," said Char and she and Booker escaped.

A frustrated looking woman in her sixties was outside the shop's front door, wrestling with a display cart. Char flashed her badge and asked, "Is this your shop?"

"It is," the woman said in an aggravated tone.

"I wonder, do you happen to live here? We were just upstairs but it didn't look like the back apartment was occupied."

"It isn't," the woman said testily. "That bastard ran off without paying the rent. I live in the back, downstairs. It's built out the back, seven rooms."

"Nice," said Char. "What we want to know is, was your tenant, Lindsay Nielsen home last night. Did you see or hear her go out or anything?"

The lady scrunched her face up. "Her? She never goes anywhere, well, not much. She is a nut case but hey, she pays the rent. I think she goes out maybe once a week. She was up there because I heard her scraping chairs around and then what sounded like dancing or stomping. Then silence. I didn't hear anybody come down the steps and I'm a light sleeper."

Back in the car, Booker said, "No sign of a hidden

kid, though that doesn't mean she couldn't have him stashed somewhere. There were two Legos on her dresser."

"Well, if that sour florist lady is correct, Lindsay didn't go out, so she'd have to have had an accomplice and what would her motive be, if no one is asking for money, to steal the kid?"

"To cause trouble?" said Booker. "But I think her mind is too focused on herself to have extra energy to commit a major crime."

Remembering her own bout with deep depression, during which she had harbored a few violent urges, Char did not comment on that.

"I have some Legos myself," she said. Though mentally, she didn't cross off the issue.

Next on the list was Carla Sarlis, the Nielsen's cleaner. She was out on a job but answered her phone and told Char where to find her. This was in a house close to Vanessa's. In fact, its owner was a social acquaintance of the Nielsens and had hired Carla at their recommendation. The cleaner answered the door.

Her employer, Carla told them, had no children, was divorced and now at the community college where she taught chemistry and other nursing courses.

Carla was in her early thirties, short, slightly chubby, and Hispanic with shiny black hair and intense brown eyes. She gave the appearance of someone who could probably run an army if called to. She led them into a brightly colored living room. "What can I do for you?" she said.

"Have you spoken with Vanessa Nielsen today?" Char asked.

Carla looked perplexed. "Well, no, it's not one of her days. I'm not due there till Thursday."

"So, you don't know then?" said Booker.

"Know what?" said Carla. Char watched her for any sign of deceit.

"The boy is missing. Caden. He wasn't in the house this morning when Mrs. Nielsen got up."

"Caden? My sweet Caden? Oh my god, no!"

"Do you have any idea where he could have gone? Everything was locked up, so whoever got into the house had to use a key."

"A key," she said thoughtfully. "I don't know. Even I don't have one. Mrs. Nielsen is usually there when I arrive and if not, I use the hidden one but not often."

"Who else knows where that is?" asked Booker.

She shook her head. "I have no idea. I'm not friends with the Nielsens, you understand. Strictly an employee, though Caden and I are fond of each other. The Nielsens have very firm ideas about social differences." Her expression was unreadable, but Char could imagine what she was not saying.

"I see," said Char. "Can we come by your house later after you're done here?"

An annoyed expression flitted across Carla's face and then vanished. "Sure, why not?" she said. "I'll be back there in a couple of hours." She gave them the address and Char and Booker left.

"Time for brunch," said Char and the two of them headed to the Spring Diner, their favorite, where each of them ordered the same thing, they always did.

"She seemed a little uptight," said Booker once he

got a good gulp of his coffee down.

"Noticed that," said Char as she stirred her tea. "No love lost for the Nielsens, though she seemed to care about the kid."

"I doubt she'd want to risk losing her job by doing anything stupid," said Booker. Looking at his phone, he said, "I did a quick check on her husband. He works for a garden center. I don't imagine he makes a high salary so she needs her position and wouldn't want to risk losing it."

Two hours later, they pulled up in front of the Sarlis house and Carla opened the door.

The home was a one and a half story bungalow from the World War II era.

"How many kids do you have?" Booker asked her.

"Three," she said. "They're at school."

"Boys, girls…?"

"Two girls and one boy," she said.

"Ages?"

"Carolina is thirteen, Leo is ten and Maya is seven."

Char stayed with Carla and made small talk while Booker did his look-around. "Who's that pretty young woman in the photo?" asked Char, choosing one out of a collection of family pictures on the wall.

Carla's expression was sphinxlike. "Ana? She's my cousin."

"What does she do?" Char asked, just to make conversation.

Carla hesitated, then replied, "She's a teacher. Well, was. She got laid off."

Char nodded and was about to move on to other photos when Booker returned, signaled an all clear, handed Carla his card and said, “Call us if anything helpful comes to mind.”

Carla nodded and they left.

“It seemed she was holding back,” said Char once they were in the car.

“Maybe someone’s green card isn’t kosher,” he said.

“Weren’t she and her husband born here?”

“I’ll look into it back at the station,” said Booker.

“Let’s do the neighbors,” said Char.

Checking with people in the Nielsens’ neighborhood yielded the information that the night before, a black, beat-up looking Chevy pickup truck was moving down the street slowly as if the driver was looking for something. The neighbor, Mr. Robert Lee, a man in his late sixties, was out walking his toy poodle around two AM. Apparently, the dog was new to his household and not properly housetrained, so, if necessary, Mr. Lee would get up and take it out.

“I thought it was suspicious,” he told the detectives. “This is a quiet street and not to sound snobby but no one who can afford to live here would be driving a vehicle like that.”

“Did you see who was in it?” Booker said.

“I think it was a woman. Didn’t get a good look but fairly sure it was.”

“Description?”

“Oh, I don’t know. Not an old one. Too quick to see details. Dark hair, I think.”

“Did the truck stop anywhere?”

“I was back at my house by then and went inside.”

Back at the station, Booker researched Carla's family (no problem there, both she and her husband were American citizens) and he and Char returned to the Nielsen's to interview Jared who had just arrived home. He looked exhausted with eyes rimmed in red and ashen skin.

"My boy," he said. "Please find him. He's everything to us." A much more personable and emotionally present person than his wife, he was not shy about expressing his feelings. Vanessa sat next to him on the sofa, stiffly on its edge and softly crying.

"First thing," said Char, settling herself into a sleek padded chair. "Are either of you familiar with anyone who drives an old black Chevy pickup truck? Have you seen one in the neighborhood?"

"Not to my knowledge," said Jared.

Vanessa, however, frowned. "Wait," she said, "I remember seeing one but when?"

She was apparently racking her brain while Char asked Jared if he knew anyone who would possibly want to harm their child or hurt the two of them for any reason.

"No," he said. "I can't imagine. I know my wife hates my sister and doesn't trust her, but I've known Lindsay way longer than Vanessa has and believe me, she's harmless. Yes, she makes scenes and is annoying, but she has never harmed anyone I know of, and she loves Caden. She doesn't spend a lot of time with him; kids just aren't her thing, but when she's here, he and she get along just fine. Sometimes he sits on her lap, and he doesn't do that with just anyone."

"Does she envy you; do you think?" asked Char.

"Well, that might be the case because we're more financially secure than she is, but we've helped her out several times and she knows we'd never let her starve."

"How about having a kid – does she envy you that?"

He shook his head. "Lindsay never wanted kids from as early as I can remember. She did not even play with dolls. I think she may even have had her tubes tied."

"She did," admitted Vanessa. "A few years back. They probably agreed to do it for her since she's nuts."

Jared shot his wife a look of disapproval.

Vanessa suddenly piped up. "I think Carla came one time in an old black pickup. Her regular car is a Kia. Dark blue. But I remember now, it was few months ago. Maybe her Kia was in the garage or something."

"You didn't ask her about it?"

"No, why should I?"

Char nodded to Booker, and they stood up. "Thank you," she said. "We'll be in touch. Try to be calm, though I know that's unlikely."

Outside, they looked at each other. "Back to Carla Sarlis," said Booker.

By now it had been over ten hours since the boy had been noticed missing. The longer it went, the less likely he would be found alive. "I have a bad feeling," said Char. "Like that the boy wasn't taken because someone wanted a kid of their own. Nor was he taken for reasons of money."

"I know what you mean," said Booker as he backtracked to Carla's house. "The boy's in danger. Funny how your gut becomes attuned in this job."

Carla opened the door immediately. She must have

seen them pull up. The kids were home now, two visible in the dining room. They walked in before she could speak.

"How many vehicles do you have?" Booker asked her.

She looked frightened now. "Well, two," she said. "My Kia and Hugo's Savana. It's white and 2012, I think. He got it used a couple of years ago."

"Okay, now," said Char firmly. "You went to work at the Nielsen's one day in an old black pickup. Whose was that?"

Her face blanched.

They waited.

"I-I had to take my car to the garage that day. Ana, my cousin, picked me up and I drove her home and then went to work in it."

"Does she still have that truck?"

"Yes."

Char moved closer. "Was Ana ever to the Nielsen's herself?"

Carla gulped. "Yes."

"Tell us about the other time or times."

"She went with me to help once. About five months ago, I think it was May. Mrs. Nielsen wanted heavier cleaning done and I said I could get my cousin to help me, that she could use the money. Ana had had a baby and was staying at her mother's, my aunt Luna's. Tia Luna said she'd watch the baby so Ana could make a little money. Her husband works on gas wells and sometimes must be away for long periods. Her baby was seven months old then."

She paused and looked off into the distance. Char had to prompt her to continue.

"The day she came with me to work, Mrs. Nielson had to go out suddenly and asked us to keep an eye on Caden. He was five then and in bed for some reason. I asked him why he wasn't getting up and he said he didn't feel good, and I noticed a rash. He said, 'Mommy's going to the farm.' I finally figured out he meant the pharmacy, so I guessed she was getting medicine for him. I didn't think much more about it. Ana sat with him a bit while I continued cleaning. Mrs. Nielson took forever coming back and I needed Ana to help me but didn't want to leave Caden alone. I tried to call Mrs. Nielsen but she didn't answer her cell. Finally, she returned with a bunch of groceries, and we finished and left. About a week later, Ana's baby got very sick, ended up in the hospital and died."

Booker said, "What about Caden? Did he get sicker?"

"It was measles, but he got over it. He was pretty sick with high fever and all. I think he even hallucinated. I wasn't afraid since I'd been vaccinated. So were my husband and kids."

"What about Mr. and Mrs. Nielsen?"

"She and her husband were vaccinated when they were kids, but she doesn't believe in vaccinations now. She lectured me a lot when I got my kids vaccinated for different things, said that can cause autism. I didn't listen to her."

Char and Booker looked at each other.

"How is Ana now?" said Char.

"She's not anything like she used to be before the baby died."

When Carla said this, her eyes opened wide, and Char knew they were all thinking the same thing.

"Can I come with you?" Carla asked.

Char hesitated and looked at Booker. This could put Carla in real danger, but she might be able to talk Ana down. "Go in your own car," Char told her. "And stay outside unless we call you in."

Carla gave them the address, which was near to her own home. Leaving off the lights and siren, the two cars pulled up in front of Ana's residence and Char called for backup. The black truck was parked in the driveway. The backup arrived in four minutes.

A knock on the front door brought no response. When the officers arrived, Booker went round one side of the house and Char the other. It was dark inside, but one light shown from what appeared to be a hallway from the kitchen. The backdoor was unlocked and they, along with four armed officers, went in. Char motioned for the officers to check the upstairs while she and Booker looked over the first floor. No one was there but a little boy's pajama top was on the floor in a corner of the kitchen.

The officers returned from upstairs. The first one shook his head.

Booker pointed at the door to the basement. An officer opened it.

Char directed one of the officers to go outside and look for another entrance into the basement. She whispered. "See what you can see in there."

"Ana?" called Char. "Are you down there?"

No answer.

"Ana? We know you're there and that you have Caden with you. We know you've suffered a great loss and we understand the rage you might feel, but please, Ana, none of it is Caden's fault. He had no say in what his mother chose to do and in fact, he himself could have died from the disease. It's not his fault. Please just let him go, let him walk up the steps."

No answer.

To Officer Styles, she said, "Get Carla out of her car and put a vest on her."

Once the woman was in the kitchen, Char had her call down to Ana. "Please, cuz, send Caden up. You know I love him. Just let me see him, please. I just want to see him."

They heard a loud sob and then the tentative tiny steps of a child as he ascended the basement steps. He stopped halfway up and looked back fearfully. He had on PJ bottoms and a Spiderman t-shirt.

"Come on, honey," said Carla. His face lit up when he saw her and he hurried up, stumbled and then at the top, Char grabbed him and pulled him to safety.

Ana, sobbing and yelling that "that bitch should have had her freakin' kid vaccinated!" was handed over to the officers and her mother, Luna, whom she had forced at gun point into the basement along with Caden, was trembling and could barely walk.

"I tried to stop her," Luna said, "but she wouldn't listen. She just wouldn't listen. Just kept saying that somebody had to pay. But she's normally a sweet girl, you don't know what she's been through, losing her baby and all. That horrible rich woman Carla works for, she killed my baby grandson. I hope she goes to hell for what she did to him and my Ana."

The older woman had held Caden the whole time, the two of them on the basement floor, faces stained with tears. And now he was back with his parents and Char and Booker were once again ensconced in their favorite booth at the Spring Diner, only this time, Char was having a martini. Not Booker though; he rarely drank.

"Ailene isn't home?" Char said once she had taken a sip of her drink with utter satisfaction.

"She went to Scranton to take some things down for Darius. Some play he's going to be in, and he needs a costume." His son had won a scholarship to a prep school there.

"She's staying overnight?"

"Yeah, with one of her college friends."

Hmmmm, Char thought to herself, but of course would not voice. She trusted Booker's wife about as far as she could throw her.

"What do you think will happen to Ana now?" Booker asked.

"Who knows?" said Char. "Psychiatric evaluation to see if she can stand trial first. I don't know if I want her in prison or a mental hospital but it's not my call anyway. What do you think she was going to do to Caden?"

He shook his head, probably thinking of his own son. "I don't even want to go there," he said.

"Evening up the score, I guess," said Char cheerfully. The drink was giving her a pleasant buzz. "And her mother? Was she going to hurt her too?"

Booker shook his head. "There is a very dark side to humanity," he said.

"That's why we have a job," said Char.

Margaret Karmazin

Margaret Karmazin's credits include stories published in literary and SF magazines, including Rosebud, Chrysalis Reader, North Atlantic Review, Mobius, Confrontation, Pennsylvania Review, The Speculative Edge, Aphelion and Another Realm. Her stories in The MacGuffin, Eureka Literary Magazine, Licking River Review and Mobius were nominated for Pushcart awards. She has stories included in several anthologies, published a YA novel, REPLACING FIONA, a children's book, FLICK-FLICK & DREAMER and a collection of short stories, RISK.

Tiny Packages

Albert N. Katz

After the insurance paid up, I had enough money to last a lifetime. What I needed was quiet and starting "Books & Co." met all my needs. That is, until that day when Howard Mitchells and Liana Zucker walked into my bookstore. Ghosts from a long-vanished past, ready to re-haunt me.

"You two looking to buy? Otherwise, get lost."

"Not a nice way to talk to your ..."

"My what? Ex-wife? And the guy she cheated with while I was recovering in hospital? That was a long time ago, OK. I forgive you if that's what you're looking for. You've got it. Now get lost."

"It's not us. It's Jimmy. He's got himself caught up in some deep shit and we don't know what to do, or where to turn."

Jimmy. James Kirkpatrick Junior. The only good

that ever came out of my time with Liana. At least I had thought so. "Jimmy? I doubt if he knows if I'm alive. Came to visit me twice. Just twice during my years in hospital and rehab. Never answers my texts. So, he needs me now? If he does, let him man up and come see me. The little prick."

"He's disappeared Jim. Like from the face of the planet. He's our child Jim. You're his Dad. I thought you'd want to help."

"Call the cops. That's what we pay taxes for."

"We can't Jim. We don't know what he was messed up with but whatever it was it was illegal. You were in special ops, know people and we thought… "

"You thought wrong. I'm just a shot-up bookseller with a prosthetic arm and leg. All my contacts are long gone. And Jimmy disappeared from my life long ago. Like I said before, Get lost."

I watch them walk away. Holding hand; Liana crying. My only thought was, dammit Jimmy what have you done now?

▼▼▼

When Jimmy had visited me in hospital the first time, he had been excited. His job was going well with some high-tech company involved in genetic consulting. The second time was just after a business trip to Asia. He was jumpy. He needed cash. Really needed it. I didn't ask questions. He just told me that he'd repay me with interest, as soon as he could. I promised him thirty K. He hugged me like he did when he was 8. "Thanks

Dad. Love you. You won't be disappointed, you'll see." I transferred the money. Received a "L U" note in return. That was five years ago. He took the cash and disappeared from my life.

▼▼▼

I may no longer be in special ops, but I had stayed in touch with some of the old gang. I make some calls. Peter Franks had been in the same ambush as I had but, in a truck, somewhat behind mine and had missed the worst of the IED. He pulled me from the flames, dodged the bullets. I owed my life to him. No longer in the forces, he was a desk jockey at the FBI, just the way he and his wife liked it.

Over espressos, I tell him about Jimmy's disappearance and his two visits to me.

"You say he was involved in a company involved with genetic consulting. Anything more?"

I shake my head, no.

"Jim, think hard. Any details at all?"

I shrug. "Something about the company was involved in cutting edge stuff. Pete, all I know is when he came to see me the second time, he seemed scared. Really scared. I think my kid has gotten himself into something over his head."

Pete gets quiet, takes out a pencil from his inner suit jacket pocket, scribbles a time and address on the paper place mat, and hands it to me. "I want you to meet Miranda Poole. She's a specialist in genetic therapies. I have a meeting scheduled with her for that time. We'll fit you in."

▼▼▼

Miranda Poole is a tall brunette with a dimple on her right cheek when she smiled. She smiles a lot. In her mid-30s, I thought, about a decade younger than me. Pete made sure when introducing her to add that she was a Full Professor, holding the Kornburg Chair of Genetics at the University, and a list of awards she had earned over her career; details that seem to embarrass and fluster her. I am introduced as "an old army buddy of mine." The two of them take turns talking.

She starts. "Jim, how much do you know about gene editing?"

"Not much. What I read. I gather there are ways to do stuff to our genes. I keep away from that stuff. Creeps me out that we might be capable of producing Frankenstein-type monsters.

She smiles. Dimple emerges. "Well, there are evermore human applications coming online for overcoming genetic disorders."

"That sounds good. So why is the FBI involved? Or, for that matter, why am I here?

"Because word on the street is that there are labs secretly doing research in the germ line."

"Germ line?"

"Modifications to genes in the sperm or egg or fetus, changes that can enter the genome of the human race, with unknown consequences."

Pete chimes in. "The agency hears that there are

labs messing around with the germ line right now, tied in with organized crime. To serve, let's say, specialized markets."

I became uncomfortable. "Such as?"

"To date we have found labs doing work for rich clients who want their children to be disease resistant or be immune from some genetic problem in their family histories, or want to ensure their child is male, blue-eyes, 6 feet tall, maybe stronger, or faster. Basically, looking for babies born to order."

That didn't sound so unusual to me. The rich always play by their own rules. "OK. So, some people want to order babies to given specs. And you think Jimmy might be involved in such activities?"

"Listen. Germ line research is legally forbidden. End of story. That's why organized crime is into it. We keep finding labs, close them down and before you know it others have popped up. So maybe Jimmy's with one of the newer ones we haven't found yet."

I get quiet.

"There is reason to believe something new, something big, something that stinks is happening under our noses. The noise out there is that it involves large-scale germ line modifications. We've even rescued a few women abducted from third world countries who were being used in lab experiments. That's when we asked Miranda to help us."

"What are you saying? That these guys are using these women as guinea pigs? As incubators?"

Both Miranda and Pete nod, in unison. "Something such as that. In some of the rescued women there were multiple changes introduced. Into the fifteenth chromosome, especially the *FGFR3* gene." When it was clear I didn't understand, Miranda points out that a mutation in that gene is associated with dwarfism.

"You think these women were being used for experiments to overcome dwarfism?"

Miranda must figure the question was pitched to her. "Quite the opposite. The manipulations were in non-mutated genes to introduce the mutation. Along with other changes we don't understand yet. Makes no sense."

"Look Jimmy has always been a bit wild but getting involved in abductions and using women in unwanted experiments, with something like this. Never. "

Pete again. "We haven't said that he was. But he might know something, and we'd like to talk to him, find out what he knows."

"Look, I've told you what I know. So can't see I can be of further use to you. Or unfortunately I can't see how this gets me any closer to finding Jimmy.'

Pete and Miranda look at each other, then Pete looks at me smiling. I thought his smile must be what a mouse sees just as the snake pounces. "I have a proposition for you."

▼▼▼

The proposition stunk. The FBI had narrowed down the field of possible laboratories capable of doing large-scale germ line editing to a handful having possible links to organized crime. What they needed was someone to get inside. They wanted me to contact possible perps with a story that I was looking for cutting edge therapy to eliminate the phantom limb pain I was supposedly experiencing ever since I lost my arm and leg.

Pete told me that if any company took the bait, I should ask for a face-to-face meeting. He is clear: "always stay as close to the truth as possible. Use your real name keep close to your real history. If the organization wants to check up on you, your army record will confirm your injuries. And don't worry; you will not wear a wire. No, one of Agencies bright guys will work out how to wire your artificial leg to use, as a transmitter.

"Pete. This is nutty. No way!"

"Do you have a better idea on how to get to the guys with whom Jimmy was likely working?"

And I didn't.

I do what they ask of me and sent out "my" letter penned by the FBI. And the waiting starts, much of it spent with Miranda teaching me about the signs that I should look for to see if illegal work was being done. I like the way she looks. thinks, smiles, smells. To my surprise, she seems to like me as well. Go figure.

▼▼▼

One after another the companies respond with "we can't help you letters". Then we hear from GeneX with a "maybe' letter. I set up a meeting with H.R. Harrison, the CEO of the company. Pete keeps reminding me that I should find out what I could about as many of their ongoing projects as possible. Miranda takes me aside, gives me a hug. Then a kiss. She is nervous. "Be careful

Jim. These might be dangerous people."

I arrive early for my appointment and am told Mr. Harrison is busy but will meet with me as soon as possible. The blond receptionist, a Miss Elizabeth Earnhardt according to the nameplate on her desk, brings me a coffee, keeps looking at me so intently that I feel uncomfortable.

H.R. Harrison laughs a lot. He reminds me more of a used car salesman than of a CEO, or scientist. I go over my practiced spiel. And he repeats much in the letter he had sent me. "As I wrote you, it's a long shot but, in theory, the line of research we are pursuing might help control your levels of pain. However, this research is still at an early stage experimental and very expensive to conduct."

I cut in. "Anything up to half a million bucks I can cover."

Harrison smiles, the same snake-eat-mouse smile I had seen in the FBI offices. "It works on mice, that we know."

"Screw mice. Can it work on me?"

"Maybe. But doing the implant on humans is currently illegal. You are young enough that you might have children after the procedure. We can't let unknown gene influences get into the human genome." He raises his arms in 'so sorry' gesture.

I try one last time. "If illegal, then I can raise my 'contribution' to one million bucks."

He hesitates, doesn't throw me out of the office. "Let me be clear. There is a large step from doing experiments with mice, then doing it with humans, even if such research were permitted."

"So, what intermediate steps are needed? It is possible if I think those steps are useful, and eventually be applied to my condition, that I might help fund that."

Harrison hesitates. "Let me make some calls to the experimental lab wing and see what they suggest. I can't promise you that we are far along in pain management research to be of use. If not, perhaps you might wish to consider funding one of our other lines of research?

I make a noncommittal, 'yes but only maybe' shrug, He asks me to leave my contact information with his receptionist. That he'd be in touch, when he gets more information from his associates. "One way or another."

When I gave the receptionist my business card for the bookstore, she offers to walk me to the elevator. On the way she looked around, and then whispers, "Are you Jimmy Kirkpatrick's father?"

She reads the answer in the shocked expression in my face. "We have to talk. It's important."

▼▼▼

Pete is ecstatic that we might have an "in" on a company possibly involved with illegal gene therapy. He is much less happy that I had offered up one million dollars of the FBI's money if needed. Miranda just looks worried.

Liz Earnhardt, Harrison's receptionist, meets me at the cafe near my bookstore, wearing sunglasses and a hat, as if that would serve as a disguise. She is clearly nervous.

"Ms. Earnhardt. Do you know where Jimmy is?"

She can't hide her disappointment, obviously hoping I would have news to tell her "Call me Liz. But no. I haven't seen him in years. When he came back from Japan and had meetings with Mr. Harrison he became really upset. Told me he'd have to lie low for a period. Left me ten thousand dollars and then just disappeared."

"Do you know why he went to Japan?"

"To meet with a potential client for GeneX. Whatever happened out there spooked him." And then, she gives me a calculating look, "Jim. Can I call you that?" I nod. "Jimmy and I had a special relationship. A very special one. And I am hoping that you and I may have one too."

I am shocked. She seems like such a nice young lady. "If you mean what I think you do. No. Not interested and besides I am old enough to be your father."

"Get your head out of the gutter and twist it around this. I have a son and you are his grandfather. Jimmy wanted the baby called James, after you. James Kirkpatrick III. If he won't have a father around, I want him at least to have a grandfather in his life. "

I am shocked. And embarrassed. Feel information overload. I am a grandfather! "My God. When can I see my grandson?"

"When I feel it's safe. Not yet. Mr. Harrison doesn't know of my involvement with Jimmy and that he's the father of my son. When I talk about my son I use his middle name, Jeremy. I want to keep it that way. I heard the angry phone calls Mr. Harrison made when Jimmy disappeared. He wants to get hold of him very badly. I am worried that he'd use us as bait to entice Jimmy out of hiding. He might be stringing you along for the same reason. Don't be fooled by his joking manner, Harrison is a scary guy."

"What in hell is Jimmy into?"

"I don't know. Jimmy was pretty tight lipped but from his reaction after his trip to Japan, nothing good you can bet."

When we part, she begs me not to call her, doesn't want to take any chance of bringing Harrison and his connections down on her. When I suggest if she is scared that she quit her receptionist job. I'd be happy to hire her to work in my bookstore. She shakes her head, answers sadly. "Can't. I owe them. You don't quit these types of guys when you're in their debt." I ask for clarification, but she clams up.

Pete and Miranda had listened into my conversation with Liz through the transmitter in my prosthetic. Miranda smiles. "So, you're a grandfather. Congratulations. I hope you can find your son." Pete's is all business, "I will phone the Public Security Agency of Japan, to see what they know. We're getting there, Jim. Step by step. We'll catch the bastards."

I don't give a shit about any of that. I had a grandson. And something like a daughter-in-law. I just wanted to find Jimmy and know that he and my new family were safe.

▼▼▼

I return to working in my bookstore while I waited to hear from Harrison. The books surrounding me no longer give me the comfort that they had before my ex-wife had walked into my shop. On the plus side, my relationship with Miranda just keeps getting better and more intimate. I am falling in love; think she is too.

Finally, I get the phone call.

When back in Mr. Harrison's office, Liz treats me indifferently, as if I were just another customer who had had one previous appointment. I interact with her in the same way.

Harrison comes straight to the point. "I just wanted to tell you in person that we could probably work on soma genes to help moderate pain levels, and that doing so might even be possibly legal. But unfortunately, we are not anywhere close to being able to do anything for you."

I start to get up. Hell, Pete could find another mole.

"Please Mr. Kirkpatrick hear me out. I have more to say"

I sit down. "Ok. Shoot."

"After you left me a few weeks ago, we checked up on you. We know you had a son. Well, he worked for me. Do you know how we might reach him?"

My shock must show but I keep my cool sufficiently to remember Pete's advice and keep my story as close to the truth as possible. "Hell no. I haven't seen him in years. Asked me for some money and after I gave it to him, he just disappeared. I'd like to get my hands on the little prick. Left me while I was recuperating in hospital."

"It is important we find him. You see he stole something from us that we must have returned. I would like you to help me find him."

Jimmy a thief? I can't believe it but then what do I know about Jimmy after all?

"And then what? You turn him over to the police. No thanks,"

"What I tell you next is private so before we continue this conversation, I have to do something." Harrison made a call and a few minutes later a burley guy walks in, asks me stand up and frisks me professionally. "He's clean Mr. Harrison." We both watch burley leave the room.

"What you hear next must not be repeated, to anyone. If any word gets out, your bookshop will be burned down and your tortured body will be found floating in the Back River, alongside those of Liz and, who knows, maybe even besides that lady you've been dating. Oh, don't look surprised. I told you we did some checking. Poor stupid Liz must think me an idiot. I've known about her and Jimmy and the kid for years."

I feel nauseous.

"Have you been working with the cops?"

Keep it close to the truth; but not to close. "Yeah. They wanted me to see if anyone might be willing to do illegal genetic therapy for me. Once I had an "in", and was trusted, they'd put a wire on me."

"Who is your contact?'

"Peter Franks. FBI. An old friend from my army days."

"Not on my pay, unfortunately. So, it is well we nipped this in the bud. Before you leave here today you will call this Franks and tell them that GeneX has looked into doing work for you but could find that their research with mice was at an early stage and there was nothing that that could be done legally, that we shook hands and I wished you goodbye and good luck. You get that?"

I nod.

"Good. Keep everything else normal. See this Peter Franks if he wants to talk, Keep dating that lady. Whatever. But don't ever discuss GeneX again. If you do, people you love will be hurt. Understand?"

I nod again.

"Good. Now let me clear about something else. You are going to be working for me. I want my merchandize returned and your job is to get it to me, whether you bring in your kid. I want to get my hands on Jimmy too, but that is secondary to the return of the merchandize. Understand?"

I nod one more time. "What is the merchandize you want back?"

"None of your frigging business. Jimmy will know. "

▼▼▼

I do, as he ordered. I call Pete and spin the story Harrison told me, while he listened in. Pete sounds surprised and disappointed. I have a sick realization while listening to the sincere regret in Pete's voice. My god, my built-in transmitter isn't working. The FBI has no clue about my situation or the danger in which I've put Miranda. I am on my own and driving blind.

Feeling trapped, I then do the other matter Harrison demanded from me. I phone the numbers he's given me of people he thought might have an interest in the merchandize Jimmy took. Following script, in each case I end my message telling the guy on the other end of the line that if they contact Jimmy he should know that I, and his girlfriend, needed to talk to him, that it is an emergency, and that he could contact me in the manner outlined in "want ad" section in the Saturday issue of the Post announcing my bookstore was looking to hire a person with a background that matched Jimmy's education and interests. I place the ad, using the number for the bookstore. I hoped that Jimmy has enough on the ball to recognize the name of the posted bookstore had been slightly changed to "Book Friends", figure something is wrong and tries to contact me on my cell phone or by some other alternative way. I just pray that Harrison has less on the ball and doesn't notice the name change.

▼▼▼

Within 48 hours my cell phone rings.

"Dad. I won't talk long. Are you and my family safe?

"For now. Harrison knows about you and Liz and your son."

There was a long silence, and then Jimmy asked, "Are you under surveillance."

"Probably."

"Shake them. Leave at night when they think you're asleep. Meet me tomorrow at 97 Conway. The door will be open."

"Jimmy, phone the number in the ad tomorrow just

after the store opens. I'll answer. Tell me on that line that you can meet me in 10 days and that you'll phone again to tell me when and where "

I want to shout out in joy. Jimmy was alive.

Jimmy does as I had asked. We have a short conversation on the store phone, ending with Jimmy telling me that he'll phone the number again when "he got closer to town." I don't know if Harrison has somehow bugged my phone but, not wanting to take a chance. I call Harrison, tell him about what Jimmy had said on the phone. Harrison sounds pleased on the other end. Too pleased.

▼▼▼

It is surprisingly easy getting out unseen, prosthetic limbs and all. No surveillance after all. Just to be on the safe side, I walk far from my house and call an Uber to take me to 309 Conway Street. I get out and when the cab has disappeared and walk to 97. Jimmy is waiting with a Talisker poured for me. We hug and very quickly get through the small talk.

"Where are Liz and my son?"

"At home. I expect. Harrison doubtless has them watched. He knows he can get them any time he wants. He probably thinks the same holds true of me. He wants what you stole really bad."

"Well, I can't do that."

"What in hell did you take?"

"Come, I'll show you?'

We walked to a bedroom in the back. A young woman was sitting in a chair reading.

"Dad, this is Juanita. She speaks pretty good English now. She's pretty smart, picked it up quickly."

"You stole a woman?"

"Look, I didn't really steal anything. It's more accurate to say I liberated her. The bastards had kidnapped her from Guatemala. Taken, as she is walking home from school. They were using her in a breeding farm they have in the countryside."

Juanita smiles at me. "You must be Senor Kirkpatrick. Your son is a good man. He saved me." And after hesitating, "because of him, my daughter was saved too."

"Jesus Jimmy, why did you ever get mixed up with these people?"

He hesitated. "The money was good. I knew they were doing something illegal when I got involved. But I thought it was just minor stuff for people with the cash to get designer babies. I really didn't know any better until I got to Japan and saw what they are doing. And then you can't leave"

"So, what in hell are they doing?"

Jimmy hesitates and then seems to decide. "They are messing with the germ line to produce babies that meet the specific desires of very rich people who don't give a damn for what they might be introducing into the human genome. Horrible stuff.

"What are you talking about?"

"I heard of a case where some perv wanted a boy-toy with a large penis, so they started looking into whether horse genes could be used. You get the picture. Harrison is servicing a market for sick people. Perverted people.

An assembly line for people who want their own very own human toys and have the money to order them.'"

I feel sick. "And they were using Juanita for this?"

"I was sent to Japan to assure one of Harrison's customers that his order was almost ready to ship. He was supposed to be extraordinarily rich, immensely powerful and very angry at the delays at our end. I hadn't an idea what the order was but was supposed to use my persuasive powers that everything was going as planned."

"When I arrived in Tokyo, two men with large tattoos, Yakuza, met me. I was blindfolded and driven to some estate in the countryside. There I met a gentleman. I never knew his name. He spoke impeccable English. He told me he was educated in Oxford, and it was in England that he started his career as a collector. He then talked extensively of the joy he gets from the exquisite beauty of the bon-zai."

"Bon-Zai?

"You know, those dwarf trees. Well, he had some. He bragged that one he bought in auction for over a million dollars. Another was reputed to be four hundred years old. But he was bored so decided what he wanted was a human bon-zai. We went into one of his rooms and there was the smallest man I've ever seen. Smaller than any dwarf, maybe sixteen inches tall, and unlike a dwarf perfectly proportioned. He told me the little guy was abnormally smart and now he wanted a female. A pair set, which he planned to mate. I hadn't an idea that was "the order" until that minute. I sweet-talked him and convinced him he would get the female bon-zoi soon."

"Jesus, Jimmy."

"What else could I do? When I got back to the States, I told Harrison that I'd not make the delivery. You can imagine how that went over. I felt trapped. Trapped by the job. Frantic with worry over Liz, who was pregnant with my own child. Harrison introduced me to Juanita, who was about five months pregnant at the time. I was ordered to take Juanita to Japan where they would oversee the final stages of gestation and the birth. When I asked Harrison whether I should bring Juanita back with me, he just told me that she's part of the package, which the customer would do with as he wished. Well after I agreed to make the delivery, I went on the lam taking Juanita with me. I used 10K of the money you leant me to give Liz some cash fall back on if needed and the rest to use to hole up."

"Where did you hole up?"

"Never ask. Any word gets out the people who helped me and their families will be killed. I will commit suicide before telling."

"Why not go the cops?"

"I'd love to but from what I've picked up, too many are on the payroll of these guys. I didn't know who to trust."

"I know a good cop. I'll call him in the morning. Harrison really wants that female bon-zai child. Where is she?"

Juanita spoke up. "When I learned what I was carrying I knew I could not let her…." She started crying.

"Dad, I came home one day to find Juanita on the bathroom floor. Blood everywhere. She had aborted her baby. I got her to a doctor who sewed her up, but she'll never be able to have children anymore."

Juanita speaks through her tears. "I know what I did, murdering my own child, is a grievous sin. I am a good Catholic Senor Kirkpatrick. I am comforted with the thought that when the day comes to answer to God, he will understand what I did was to save my child from a life of slavery and perversion, and that he will have compassion for me, send me to purgatory and not hell."

Before I could say another word, two burley guys break into Jimmy's flat, with guns pointing at us. Burley #1 was succinct. "Mr. Harrison wishes to see you."

▼▼▼

We are driven for quite a while, ending up in what looked like a factory, led into to a large storage room. Inside were Liz and James Kirkpatrick III, the last asleep in a makeshift bed. It is the first time I had seen my grandson. I fear it will be the last. He looks so much like Jimmy did at that age. Liz is crying. Harrison has the look of the cat ready to feast on the canary. "Come in gentlemen, Juanita, just in time to join the party."

Liz and Jimmy run to each other, hug and kiss. Harrison just looks at them sardonically. "You amateurs are so fucking stupid. Jim, did you actually think I missed the change to the name of your bookstore in the ad or ever think I'd have a professional tail on you or fall for the b.s. in the phone call about meeting in 10 days? You should have listened to me when I explained the fate of those who cross me."

I thought it was my time to say something but all that

came out was, “You’ll never get away with this.” Harrison laughs. “I think I’ve heard that line in a thousand second-rate films. Come, let me show you something.”

Harrison and the Burleys lead us further into the building. There were many small rooms, with glass doors, behind which woman were asleep or looking blankly at us as we passed. “Do you remember this place, Juanita? You spent many months here while we were preparing you for your trip to Japan. I see you shaking my dear. I guess this doesn’t bring back pleasant memories.” He points vaguely to the right. ‘Over there we do our gene editing.” He points to the left, “Over there we have our animal labs, mostly mice but some primate too. Impressive, no”

We end up in front of a metal door, and Harrison drawing a pistol, ushers us through it. It clangs shut behind us. The room is furnished with a couch, coffee table and desk. Oil paintings hang on the wall. He sits behind the desk leaving the rest of us standing. “This is my favorite room, my oasis from the bustle of everyday nastiness. It is serene yet perfectly soundproof and completely secure. But I am not here to talk about interior design. No, today it is about the necessities of everyday nastiness.” He turns to Juanita and Jimmy, waving his pistol around. I calculate the likelihood of jumping him but realize we are all too far away.

“Here is what is going to happen. Juanita, Jimmy, you cost me a lot of money. When the package failed to show up in Japan the buyer was unhappy; very unhappy. I couldn’t very well start a war with the Yakuza, so I sent him another bon-zai girl. But of course, this was sent o be my gift. Because of the loss of face, he endured I also promised that I would send him both your heads as soon as I could. It will be a relief to me that debt will soon be paid. But let me assure you that your deaths will not be quick nor painless" Looking directly at Juanita, "I was hoping to recover some of those funds spent on my gift to our Japanese customer by selling a later child you bear for us, but alas paying off the debt takes precedence."

"You're a monster Harrison. "

"Actually, Jimmy, I prefer to think of myself as a businessman A successful businessman."

It is clear he is relishing targeting each of us, one by one. "Liz, you are really an idiot. After we did that little favor, you begged us to do for you and fixed your son's genetic abnormality that would have caused him to die *in utero*, did you not even imagine once that I would *not* know that Jimmy was the father? We do genetic mapping research after all! I know more about his genetic make-up then you ever will. Given your betrayal in not disclosing your relationship with Jimmy, I have decided that you will end up in one of those little glass door rooms, serving the greater good of GeneX research. Some of our failed experiments turn out to be quite painful to the woman involved. I cannot promise that you will be spared that fate. As for your kid, know his special talents will be of use to GeneX and me. He'll grow up as my son. You and Jimmy will not be a blip in his memories."

"Bastard", I screamed as I started to lunge at him, but stopped when he pointed his gun at me. "Jim, such language and in front of your grandson! Well, you already know your fate. Your dead, tortured body thrown into the Back River. I have not yet decided whether your girlfriend will join you. Nothing personal you know. It is just I can't let people think they can cross me without consequences. Ah, decisions. Decisions. Well, let us not tarry then. You each have your destinies to meet" He goes to an intercom, "George. Pytor, can you please come in? I have some jobs for you," and pushes a buzzer to release the door lock.

The door slowly swings open. Pete Franks and an army of FBI agents rush in. With the door open, we hear gunshots and screams. Harrison looks stunned, drops his gun, and lifts his hands in surrender.

All I could think of was another banal line from a thousand films. "What took you so long?"

Pete smiles wryly. "Never told you, but our whiz kinds not only put a transmitter into your prosthetic but a direction finder as well. We've had you under 24/7 surveillance ever since you phoned with that cock-and-bull story about Harrison not willing to help. Couldn't inform you of course or we'd blow our surveillance. We just didn't want to pounce until we knew the whereabouts of the underground gene editing and breeding facility. "

"Jesus and Mary. We could all have been killed."

His smile was snake-like again. "But you weren't"

▼▼▼

Life goes on. The rich and powerful stay rich and powerful. The little guys get punished or, in Pete's case, a modest promotion. The GeneX lab has been closed down and some guys prosecuted. However, I know more dark labs will spring up. That's the way of nature. It abhors a vacuum. Harrison, the bastard, will live his life with a new name under the witness protection program. I hope he spends his life looking over his shoulders afraid that hit man will find him.

The Yakuza leader has not been identified and I suspect will not be. All we know is that he has a mating pair of bon-zai humans. Miranda thinks it is unlikely their gene mutations will enter the general human genome unless egg implantations or sperm donations are used. But who knows for sure? Frankly I'm scared sick about what is happening out there. Miranda thinks it more likely that, if the bon-zai couple can produce viable offspring, a new species of humans could emerge over time. When I mention my concerns, Pete just dismisses it. "So what? They're only inches tall, for God Sake." I kept on thinking that viruses are small but deadly, and of the Yakuza boss telling Jimmy that his bon-zai boy was abnormally smart. I wonder what the first Neanderthals must have thought when they saw their first, oh-so-weak, Homo sapiens.

As for me? Well, Miranda and I have been talking about getting married. I've had the FBI whiz kids remove the transmitter and whatever other junk they put into my prosthetic. I want my privacy and, sure as hell, neither Miranda nor I want people listening in on our bedroom activities. I like the feel of her next to me the last thing at night and the first in the morning. Even so, often I find it hard to fall asleep. I lie there listening to her deep-sleep breathing, replaying Harrison's words indicating that my grandson's had "special talents", wondering what other changes they made to his DNA and the human germ line.

Shark's Blood

Karen Keeley

The two gorillas flanking me made it impossible to slap that ugly grin from Ed Gallagher's face no matter how lofty my aspirations. Gallagher had me over a barrel, a definite disadvantage. He'd caught me coming onto the property bold as brass, acting like I owned the joint.

I knew of its location, its reputation, a non-descript warehouse located in a seedier part of Vancouver right on the waterfront at the foot of Columbia Street. Prior to my arrival, I'd had to wait for two trains shunting back 'n forth before I could cross over, my little psychedelic VW bug put-puttin' like a teakettle while watching more than eighty boxcars rumble past.

Gallagher too, was well known amongst Vancouver's seedier element, a procurer of illegal goods in the guise of stolen automobiles, usually a Bentley or a Rolls

Royce taken from some affluent neighbourhood. He dummied-up their vehicle registrations, their VIN numbers skewed. The vehicles were then driven across the border at night, down near Aldergrove where the cops tended to run thin on the ground.

The cops were also running thin on the ground when it came to finding Linda O'Leary, a fifteen-year-old gone missing twelve hours earlier. That was due to the fact Linda's old man, Shane O'Leary had steered clear of the cops, hired me instead.

It was no secret O'Leary and Gallagher were enemies, rivals in the nefarious business of crime. Initially, Linda's father, Shane O'Leary found me in the yellow pages. What was secret, O'Leary and I were family, he and my mother siblings but I'd never actually met the man until that morning to discuss Linda's recovery. When my parents married, my mother became a Shark. I rather liked our surname. And me, I'd never married, at least not yet. Given the women's lib movement, it seemed unlikely wedding bells would ring anytime soon. The idea I could burn my bra whenever I wanted, that too, gave me clout. Too bad, Gallagher didn't see it that way.

"O'Leary wants his daughter back." I reached inside the suede drawstring bag I used as a purse and brought out a picture of Linda O'Leary. She was a cute kid, just turned fifteen and wanting to look like Twiggy, that pixie-styled haircut with the big black eyes, the exaggerated eyelashes and the pale lipstick. I too, was a flaxen blonde but I tended to run more Arlo Guthrie, the wild and crazy locks with a life of their own, the reason for the Arlo Guthrie hat, my signature trademark.

"Too bad about the kid," said Gallagher. He'd been smoking a cigarette when I first entered the warehouse. He snuffed the last of it in a metal ashtray, his counterfeit smile drying up like a shrivelled raisin. "I got kids of my own. Maybe she ran off, a guy like Shane O'Leary for a father."

"According to O'Leary, his kid is a good kid, not one to run off. Someone took her, snatched her off the street coming home from a babysitting job. He thinks it was you."

"The guy's got imagination, I'll give him that." Gallagher now looked mean.

I pocketed Linda's picture in a jacket pocket, a spiffy number I'd found at Woodward's. The downtown department store carried everything a girl could want in clothing and cosmetics along with legitimate Sony transistor radios and those Princess telephones all the girls were raving about, not the counterfeit knockoffs Shane O'Leary was into.

"O'Leary hired me as the go-between," I said. "You give me the kid; you get what you want."

"What I want," repeated Gallagher. He rubbed his chin, freshly shaved just that morning. I had to give it to the guy. He never looked shabby despite the business he was in, tailor-made suits cut from a good cloth. I imagined he was a hard fit, a big guy like him, well over six feet tall and pushing two forty on the scales. "I take it you didn't have to burn your bra to get your PI license," he said. "City Hall too, getting in on the action, supporting women's lib."

"Forget women's lib. I came because of O'Leary's missing kid."

"The jacket, very nice." Gallagher was obviously toying with me. "You do the ensemble justice, Miss Shark—or may I call you Alex?"

That surprised me. I hadn't told him my name.

"Yeah, I know who are," he sneered. "If you were a man, I'd say private dick but why be rude to a lady? I like the white turtleneck, sleeveless, right? The kind the wife likes—that and the mini-skirt, the boots and the hat. Same kind Arlo Guthrie wears, am I right again?"

"I'm surprised you know who Arlo Guthrie is," I told him.

"I get around. We got radios—even in this dump," and he laughed. "I gotta hand it to O'Leary. He's into a lucrative venture, the electronics, the radios and those Princess telephones. What kid doesn't want one of those? I got two girls at home, both squirrely for those phones, telling me, they're rad, they're mod." He drummed his fingers on his desk. "I ask you, what kind of language is that? You'd think those goddamn phones were the second coming the way they light up in the dark."

"And what about you, working in the dark, something else you're good at," I said.

"That's my business," Gallagher growled. "I also make it my business to know what the competition is up to, especially when horning in on my patch."

"How's that?" I asked, taking a gander around the seedy office at the back of the warehouse, wondering where he had Linda stashed.

Gallagher leaned back in his chair, lit up another of

his smelly cigarettes, a Player's Navy Cut, a filthy habit but most everyone was doing it, including indulging in a toke of skunkweed now and then.

He told me what I already knew, Shane O'Leary setting up shop near Gallagher's warehouse, giving law enforcement a reason to come sniffing around, not good for business. O'Leary imported his knockoffs from somewhere in Southeast Asia, the contraband smuggled into Canada in containers of phosphorus. Whoever O'Leary sold to; they didn't seem to care about the provenance of the items. They simply resold what they'd scored with a fifty, sixty percent markup, like what Gallagher did with his luxury automobiles.

"I hear O'Leary greases the palms of a couple of dock workers connected to the port authorities," said Gallagher. "The phosphorous then used in the making of fertilizer. But we both know different, don't we? Fertilizer can be used for explosives, and explosives are big business, too. You tell O'Leary, he comes onto my patch, I want in. After that, he then gets his kid back."

I stepped forward. The two gorillas on either side matched me. "He gets his kid back and then I tell him."

"And what's to stop him from reneging?" growled Gallagher, studying the growing length of the ash on the end of his smoke.

"We both know if you grabbed Linda once, you'd do it again. O'Leary won't bargain with his kid's life."

Gallagher laughed. "You sound certain on that."

I nodded. "I am," and left it at that, no need to mention my blood tie to the competition. "Give me Linda and I'll take her home. I give O'Leary your demands for her safe return. He's willing to deal."

"Willing to deal. Hmm—wish he'd said that a week ago." He took a final drag off his smoke, snuffed it out in the ashtray, stood tall, shoulders squared. "We could've saved ourselves a lot of trouble, especially for his kid."

I took another step forward, overplayed my hand. The two gorillas each grabbed an arm, pulled me back. There was talking to the boss and then there was threatening the boss. Even for a woman, sometimes I can look and act damn threatening despite the boots, the mini skirt, the leather jacket and the Arlo Guthrie hat.

"So, you do have her," I said.

"You tell O'Leary I want a thirty-percent cut on his next shipment."

I bit my bottom lip, tried to look thoughtful. "First the girl. Where is she?"

Gallagher gave a slight nod of the chin, that universal signal for one of the two big apes flanking me to go and fetch the girl. The big gorilla returned a couple of minutes later with Linda, dragging her along by an arm. The kid was a fighter, kicking him in the shins.

Somewhere along the way she'd torn her school uniform, a mini-length pleated plaid jumper, a white blouse and a knitted cardigan. She'd lost her school tie. Her fishnet stockings were ripped at the knees and her suede desert boots too, had taken a beating. I found out later, she'd been held in a locked washroom with a couple of stalls, a rusty sink and a broom closet holding cleaning supplies. Her smudged mascara and eyeliner soiled her cheeks, an obvious sign of crying. There was no sign of any lipstick. I figured she'd bitten all of that off while crouched on the floor, her knees hugged tight to her chest, all the while wondering—what next?

"Get her some water," I snarled, going to her, offe-ring her a tissue squirreled at the bottom of that draws-tring bag.

The big ape who retrieved Linda left and soon re-turned with a bottle of Coca-Cola, possibly from the vending machine I'd spied when I'd first entered the warehouse.

Linda drank it down like a parched camel, draining it in one go, barely breathing.

I took off my jacket, soft cowhide, and wrapped it around her shoulders. "My name is Alex Shark," I told her. "I'm going to take you home to your father."

"Not him," she whispered, wiping dribbled Coke from her chin. "It's because of him they took me. Can you take me to my mom?"

"Aren't they living together?" Her father had neglec-ted to share that bit of information. Maybe he thought if I knew about the separation that would somehow sabo-tage the return of his daughter.

Linda shook her head. "Mom left him weeks ago. She's had enough, him and his criminal activities. My father's a first-class jerk just like that sicko sitting there." She nodded her chin at Gallagher.

Ed Gallagher laughed—a deep baritone. "I like the kid. She's got spunk."

Because of the laughter, I took a flying leap across the desk and managed to land one good slap across the left side of his ugly mug before his two henchmen grab-bed me. There was nothing lady-like about my actions.

I was hauled back across the desk and slapped silly for good measure.

Linda too, had taken a swing at one of them, using the Coke bottle as a weapon, about as harmless as a fly sparing with the current heavy-weight title holder, smokin' Joe Frazier. Like Gallagher had said, the kid had spunk.

Eventually, set free, I grabbed Linda, squared my Arlo Guthrie hat and we headed for the door. I turned in the doorway, wiped blood from my split lip. It was going to hurt like hell in a couple of hours and ruin any attempt to apply lipstick, always overrated in my opinion but a girl's got to look the part, sophisticated and classy.

"Your vehicles," I said. "All part of your ill-gotten gain. A different kind of steel sold south of the border. Care to elaborate?" Linda had grabbed my jacket from off the floor, having dropped it during the scuffle. She handed me the used tissue, the one I'd given her earlier. I dabbed at my bleeding lip.

Gallagher laughed. "A different kind of steel, I like that. Yeah—I steal 'em and make one hell of a profit. But you already know that you and the kid. I suggest you keep that knowledge to yourself."

"Just another businessman," I sneered, wishing I had gotten in two more slaps before his thugs slapped me silly like a ragdoll.

"And now expanding thanks to O'Leary, him and me business partners."

Linda too, sneered. "My father will see you rot before he deals with the likes of you."

Gallagher laughed again. "Like I said, the kid's got

spunk. Now get outta here before I change my mind and you're both delivered to Vancouver General on stretchers. Some people's kids—can't live with 'em, can't live without. Just like the goddamn wife."

Crossing the railway tracks, headed west on Cordova toward North Vancouver, Linda asked, "What did you mean about his cars sold south of the border? What's that jerk-face up to?"

"I need to get you home," I told her. "Your old man is expecting you. I know—I said I'd take you to your mom, and I will. But first to your father. He's the one who's paying me."

"Paying you?"

"I'm a private investigator, kid. I'm a finder of lost items. You were lost."

Her thin white hand, wraithlike, held the empty Coke bottle. "Did you know you can make Molotov cocktails out of these things?"

I took my eyes off the road for a second or two, swivelled my head like it was on a spit. "Jesus, kid. Where'd you hear that?"

"Television. The peace rallies in the States. That's what you're referring to, isn't it? It's been on the news. Protesters shot at that university in South Carolina. And then Martin Luther King getting shot when all he wanted was a peaceful march. Maybe now that Robert Kennedy is gonna run for the presidency, things will get better."

"You're fifteen. How the hell do you know all this shit?"

"All this shit is my world," said Linda. "That and what I live with, a father who's a criminal."

She had me there. Her father was a criminal. "I don't know that Bobby Kennedy will make much difference," I told her. "But he's gonna try. There are a lot of people upset by too much political upheaval, social and civil injustices, race relations gone wild and the conflict in Vietnam," which begged the question, how was O'Leary managing to secure those barrels of phosphorous, a bloody war killing far too many on both sides. I knew, like most everyone who watched the nightly news, North Vietnam had ties to the Soviet Union and the Soviet Union had ties with China. Was O'Leary getting his knockoff electronics from China? Whatever his game, I didn't need to know the details. There was enough unrest to worry about at home.

"The conflict is happening here too," I said, "in our country."

I shifted gears, my little psychedelic bug labouring as it climbed a steep hill.

"The FLQ, that Front de libération du Québec terrorist group. It wouldn't surprise me if they kidnapped or killed some high ranking official and Pierre Elliott Trudeau, our illustrious leader of the political mod-squad is gonna have to invoke the War Measure Act."

Linda thought about what I'd said but stayed quiet. Then, "I hate my life," as she toyed with the empty Coke bottle. "A criminal for a father and everyone knows it, the bullying at school, no friends, no fun. There's nothing but crapola on TV. I think the future is fucked."

"Jesus, kid—don't say that. Nice young ladies shouldn't use language like that."

"I'm not a nice young lady. I'm Shane O'Leary's

daughter, remember?"

"Your father loves you, he told me so."

Was this the time to tell her we were related? Knowing her father, he too, would slap me silly, reminding me blood may be thicker than water but that didn't give me the right to blow the whistle on the family blood ties. He and my mother hadn't seen each other in years.

"Of course, he'd say that," spat Linda. "All fathers mouth the words but when it comes to putting it into action, they fall short. I never would've been snatched off the street if he'd truly loved me, put my welfare first."

She had a point there. "The reason I want to go to my mom's. At least she tries."

"Did they treat you okay?" I asked.

"Yeah, they were okay. They fed me if that's what you mean. And they gave me a couple of blankets. Everything smelled like petrol. I couldn't sleep though, not knowing if help would come. Thank you—is it missus or Miss Shark?"

"Alex, please. It has a nicer ring to it." I offered her a smile.

"Alex, I like it. Is it short for Alexandra?"

"It is. I was named after my father."

"Was he a nice man? A good man?"

"He was a cop. Killed in the line of duty."

I swallowed the conflicting emotions that rose whenever I thought of my old man, him a cop which meant he'd believed in corporal punishment, his favourite weapon of choice, a leather belt across the back of my legs. Had that meant he'd cared? Better to remember the good times rather than the bad.

"I thought about becoming a cop," I told her. "To do that, I'd've had to break glass ceilings. I'm not the break-glass-ceilings kind of gal. As a private investigator, I can at least throw stones at those living in glass houses, try to get their attention."

Linda laughed. "I like you, Alex Shark. You're my kind of woman."

I had no idea what she meant by that but at least she was laughing following her ordeal. She then got quiet. "I hope my father is paying you well."

"Not your concern," I said. "Let's get you home, and then to your mother's."

What followed was me thinking everything was copacetic when a week later Shane O'Leary called in an uproar. "The bastard! He's done it again. Linda's gone!"

"Whaddya mean she's gone?" I shuffled paperwork, five years of tax returns spread across my desk, the current job, a forensic accounting blunder, looking for signs of embezzlement. I told O'Leary I had left Linda at her mother's, like she'd wanted. "I dropped her there a week ago."

"Her mother just called," O'Leary growled. "Linda didn't come home from school today. Evelyn is frantic. Christ—why do women automatically erupt with supersonic ferocity when it comes to their kids? Come and get me, we're going to Gallagher's and this time I'll confront him myself."

I shovelled the tax returns into a filing cabinet and scooted on over to O'Leary's home in North Van, pushing my little VW bug into the red zone, its engine labouring once again climbing the steep hills. The vehicle may have stood out in a crowd, psychedelic yellow with its colourful decals, but it didn't have the horsepower of a Bentley or a Rolls Royce. What it did have was anonymity. When working a job, most folks thought I belonged to the press, some cub-reporter looking for a story which was fine by me.

I picked up O'Leary, him spittin' nails. I didn't stay long enough to admire the Andy Warhol prints hung on the walls or the colourful PVC lampshades most likely purchased at Woodward's by the wife now taking an unscheduled sabbatical. We high-tailed it to Gallagher's warehouse and got stuck on the south side of the tracks for a good ten minutes, those damn trains shunting back 'n forth. O'Leary couldn't get comfortable in the VW bug. How could he? He too, was a big man and not meant for small spaces. His knees were crowding the dash, shoved up tight against the glovebox. That compromised my ability to grab my snub-nosed revolver should a snub-nosed revolver be required, but considering O'Leary was family—I was hoping the requirement for a firearm wouldn't be necessary.

I'd barely managed to park when O'Leary jumped clear of the little bug and took off running, his snappy Florsheim wingtips slapping the mud. I followed, my snappy PVC go-go boots tapping out a snappy rhythm which had me thinking of Arlo Guthrie's *Alice's Restaurant* just a half mile from the railway tracks. Singing protest songs had to be easier than battling crime.

O'Leary pulled out his revolver, a big ugly thing. "Put that away," I snarled. "If Linda is here, bullets ricocheting off the concrete walls won't help. Not if we're dead."

O'Leary holstered the revolver under his Italian sport jacket. I knew then he'd been watching one too many Cagney movies which probably began when he was a punk kid constantly at loggerheads with his old man, according to my mom.

Inside the warehouse, he hollered, "Where is she?" Two vehicles were parked against the far wall, a furniture van and a Bentley, a beautiful number, midnight blue, a custom order, a custom job, with its shiny chrome and white-wall tires. I had to give it to Gallagher—he knew his stuff when it came to luxury vehicles.

He came from the back room, his two henchmen with him. "Where's who?" he growled.

O'Leary shouted, "Linda, you bastard! You're a double-crossing loud-mouth piece of shit!"

"I haven't got her, you lowlife good-for-nothing weasel!"

Like I said, rivals in all things which now included name calling.

"Why would I have your kid?" hollered Gallagher. "I got what I wanted. Your pet pooch in the Arlo Guthrie hat delivered the goods last week, the electronics and the phosphorus—a lovely glow in the dark. Nifty stuff that phosphorous."

He nodded to his two henchmen. They circled around; revolvers drawn from their shoulder holsters. This was going to get ugly fast.

"If you don't have Linda," I said. "Then we'll be leaving." I pulled O'Leary's arm, made him back up two, three steps, slow like. "There's been a misunderstanding and we extend our apologies."

"That's more like it," said Gallagher. "Now scram."

O'Leary didn't come easy. Spittle flew from his lips like a rabid dog as I pulled him along in my wake. Once we were clear of the warehouse, I yanked him around back behind a dumpster. "She's there, but Gallagher doesn't know she's there," I told him.

"Whaddya mean?" snarled O'Leary. "Jesus, Alex—she's family, your goddamn cousin!"

"I know, and she's playing hero." I straightened my nifty hat on my head. "I saw her school bag lying near the far wall, in the shadows. It appears Gallagher's making that delivery tonight, most likely the Bentley squirreled away in that furniture van, it too, likely stolen. We wait and we follow. Your daughter is trying to right your wrongs. I think she's hidden herself in the trunk of the Bentley. Somehow, she's going to make herself known to the authorities once they cross the border at Aldergrove. She's expecting her perceived kidnapping will nail Gallagher to the proverbial cross."

"Christ!" whispered O'Leary. "You spotted her school bag. What if Gallagher sees it?"

"He'll think it was dropped when they snatched her a week ago. It's not like they've got a cleaning crew on site. Gallagher's two henchmen, I doubt they're familiar with soap and water."

O'Leary scrubbed his face, a father deeply hurting. "If you're so sure she's in there, then we go get her."

I grabbed his arm a second time. "I got a better idea. Follow me and shut up."

"Jesus—you're as bossy as your mother," he

growled.

"She learned it from you. She says to thank you, by the way."

"Thank me?"

"Because of you she married my father. She said marrying a cop kept her out of trouble, she could sleep nights. It was a lot less stressful than living with a bunch of bandits."

"We weren't bandits," snarled O'Leary.

"According to her, you were. Your old man into bootlegging back in the day."

"Christ! Everyone was into bootlegging. That's what you did when the well ran dry."

"Like robbing banks when the money runs dry."

"Okay, very funny. You're crackin' me up."

"Good. A bit of humour lightens the load. Now—follow me."

Back at my office downtown near the Cambie Street Bridge, O'Leary was all for forming his own posse, get a couple of his own henchmen together and they could duke it out with Gallagher's gorillas in the warehouse. Like I said—too many Cagney movies. It was all I could do to get him to sit tight while I made my phone calls, orchestrating a plan for the safe return of Linda while nailing Ed Gallagher to that proverbial cross.

Hours later, the plan in place, it was going on for ten o'clock when we watched Gallagher and his cronies drive out of the warehouse. Whoever was driving had failed their exam, the sound of grinding gears downright wretched. Earlier I'd snuck up to a window, taken a peek, and yeah—the Bentley was safely stored within the van.

It would take an hour for them to get to the border, a dirt tract crisscrossing a farmer's field which straddled both sides of the international boundary line at Avenue Zero out in the valley.

Prior to the drive, O'Leary balked at climbing into my VW bug. "You expect me to fold myself into that thing again—like a sardine?"

"Think of your daughter. You owe her." I turned the ignition key. "We're not taking your limo. It's a goddamn Cadillac. Gallagher would spot it a mile away, even in the dark."

"Christ!" He'd folded himself in, grousing about having to spend an hour or more in a sardine can, unable to move. I smiled, told him that's what you did. Made sacrifices for family.

Now I hung back, stayed out of sight. It wasn't hard to spot the big furniture van in the dark, traffic was light. My VW bug however, resembled a Monarch butterfly so keeping my distance was imperative.

Earlier, I'd been in touch with Lou Adams, my father's former partner. Adams had moved up through the ranks, now a Deputy Chief Constable. I knew he'd have a crackerjack team in place, working with the border guards, both Canadian and US.

It was pitch black, only the van's headlights lighting up the dirt tract, thick brambles and bushes bordering either side of Avenue Zero. Gallagher had obviously done the trip before. Whoever was driving showed no hesitation slowing for potholes. The furniture van swayed like an old barge heaving fore and aft on an uneasy sea.

Just after eleven o'clock the van crossed the international border and that's when all hell broke loose. A battery of floodlights snapped on; the area lit up like Area 51 in a dry Nevada desert. All we were missing were the oval-eyed Martians with their ray-guns.

One of the US border guards approached the van, his firearm drawn and held at the ready. A half dozen more circled the truck. They too, were loaded down with firepower.

"All of you in the vehicle—please step out." It was nice to hear he was polite as well as officious and business-like.

Gallagher and his henchmen did as he asked. "What seems to be the problem?" asked Gallagher, tossing a cigarette butt into the dirt, him now spittin' nails.

The guard reached into the van, took the key out of the ignition and swung open the tailgate. He shone a flashlight inside. He then jumped up, found the key to the Bentley in its ignition and used that to open the trunk. That's when I made my appearance from the bushes. O'Leary remained hidden, no need for him to get directly involved and Linda popped up out of the trunk. She was rubbing her eyes, saw me, and jumped clear. She ran to me, threw her arms around my waist.

"Illegal entry and kidnapping," stated the US border guard. "That'll about do it, boys. Take both vehicles apart—let's see what else we can find."

I held Linda close, handed her a flashlight, whispered she should take a discreet peek into the bushes, she'd see her father hiding. To then follow the dirt tract back to my VW parked a quarter mile behind me, to meet her father at the car. Linda took off like a Jack rabbit, never looking back.

Lou Adams was with the Canadian contingency. He gave me a hearty handshake, said it would be a lucrative bust, the alleged kidnapping in addition to the illegal contraband they expected to find in the Bentley, the vehicle stolen a month back. The furniture van too, had been swiped the day before. Two of Adams' boys were busy snapping photos, a bevy of flashbulbs exploding, all part of the evidence gathering.

If looks could kill, Gallagher would've had me filleted into shark steaks. "I should've known it would be you," he snarled. Two US border guards stood on either side of him. "You were seen earlier this evening circling the warehouse like a goddamn shark. I told my guys to let it go, that you'd probably dropped an earring the other day, you'd come back to look for it."

"Not an earring, Gallagher. I was circling for blood."

He lunged, tried for a slap on the face. Lou Adams grabbed his wrist, kept him from doing further damage to my already split lip, now healing nicely. The border guards led Gallagher away, his two gorillas too, in custody. Gallagher was busy talking up his rights, he wanted his lawyer. I had no idea who that was and didn't care.

The Bentley didn't disappoint. In a false bottom in the trunk, under where Linda had lain, they found four containers of phosphorous destined for explosive use, knowing Gallagher, a way to put a decisive bang into a peaceful protest march or a civil rights campus sit-in providing those using it could work the formula properly. It was finicky stuff that phosphorous. There were also numerous cartons of counterfeit electronics stored in the van, including the Princess telephones that were all the rage, stacked and corded, the delivery I'd orchestrated the week before.

Lou Adams looked around for Linda, realized she'd high-tailed it for my little VW bug. He told me to take her home, he'd stop by in the morning to get a statement.

I joined O'Leary and Linda at my vehicle. I hugged Linda close, gave her skinny shoulders a squeeze. "You were one brave girl," I said. "Stupid, but brave."

Linda laughed. She wore a navy pea-coat over hip-hugger bell-bottoms and a tie-dyed tee-shirt. Her suede desert boots were speckled with mud. "I'm glad you figured it out."

"Me too," and then I asked her, "How did you know they were moving the Bentley?"

"A fly on the wall," she said. "I heard them talking when I was locked in that washroom, the heating vent. I thought they were gonna cross at the Peace Arch. When the truck stopped, I'd scream bloody murder, hoping someone would hear and rescue me, the jerk face arrested for kidnapping."

I gave her skinny shoulders another squeeze. "You and me, we're good?"

"You know we are." She smiled. "We're cousins. Family sticks together."

So, O'Leary had shared that bit of news after all, neglecting to inform me, not cool. What was cool, we were family. "How does that make you feel?"

"Groovy!" said Linda, and then, "Shark—is that your real name? Or is it a pseudonym you took on when you became a private investigator?"

“It’s my real name,” I told her, tossing my car keys, a sign it was time to go. “One I’d gladly share with you. Shark’s blood, known for its stealth-like qualities. From now on, you’re Linda “the Shark” O’Leary. Let the bullies at your school deal with that.”

Linda climbed into my psychedelic bug and got comfortable in the backseat. O’Leary climbed in, pulled his knees up to his chin. He kept grousing about the confined space, why would anyone want to own a goddamn beetle? It was uncivilized. “I’m getting too old for this cockamamie shit,” he growled.

Linda reached over from the backseat and hugged him, kissing him repeatedly on the ear, that annoying fly she’d alluded to. I’d set the brim of my hat at a rakish angle; glad I’d tossed the bobby pins back in high school. Since becoming a bona fide gumshoe, I’d embraced my wild and crazy side, including the flaxen curls, them and the hat my signature look, but unlike Guthrie who rebelled against the establishment with his protest songs, and because I was a lady, I wasn’t gonna burn the bra just yet—I needed all the support I could get.

Karen Keeley

Karen Keeley first fell in love with a good who-done-it when she stumbled upon Rex Stout and his *Nero Wolfe* novels at a used bookstore in Thunder Bay, Ontario, her go-to resource when looking for inspiration for her own writing. Her story *Crying all the way to the bank* was one of the winners in the international short story competition *Round Midnight* (Strange Day Books). Other stories have appeared in numerous anthologies, the most recent *Born under a Bad Sign* (Screaming Eye Press). A forthcoming story will appear in *Women of a Certain Age,* a Canada West Anthology October 2022. She makes her home in Calgary, Alberta, Canada.

The Curious Marriage of Simon Woodburn

Renee Lehnen

Simon Woodburn couldn't recall the exact moment he realised he was a cuckold. The scales had fallen slowly from his eyes, as if he were gradually sharpening the focus on a telescope, or clearing the ice from a windshield, squirt and swipe, squirt and swipe, though the signs of his wife's infidelity had flashed in neon. They lived together, seemingly content, Simon pretending he didn't know, and Grace pretending she didn't know that he knew. He couldn't go on like this. Not now.

Simon arrived at the East Elmington Public Library at quarter past eight, forty-five minutes prior to opening, when he would unlock the great oak doors at the top of the broad stone stairway. Simon always arrived a half-hour before the other staff. He cherished the spacious quiet, the vanilla smell of paper and paste and old wood, and the order. Soon patrons would spill through the doors holding clandestine throwaway coffee mugs under their jackets, pulling mucousy children behind them, and marking the floor with muddy footwear.

As on every other weekday morning, Simon entered the granite building by the staff entrance, changed from his New Balance walkers to his loafers, hung up his overcoat, clipped his name tag onto the left pocket of his shirt, and put his lunch, contained in stacked Tupperware, into the staff fridge. Then, whistling some half-remembered show tune, he playfully swung his lanyard of keys and strolled to the after-hours book return. Apart from rare occasions when he'd find a Doritos wrapper, or worse, Simon relished the daily slice-of-Christmas moment when he unlocked the back of the receptacle box to discover what'd tumbled in overnight. "Who could ask for anything more?" hummed Simon.

He pulled the door open, leaving the keys hanging from the lock. Then, he pushed a metal basket against the bottom edge of the box with his right knee and carefully scooped DVDs, CDs, magazines, picture books, novels in paper and hard cover- a representation of all the Elmington Public Library system featured on its shelves- into the basket. Last in was a dog-eared *Penthouse* magazine.

Strange, thought Simon. The library doesn't subscribe to *Penthouse.* Someone must've mixed up his own magazine with the library's.

Simon locked the book box door and heaved the basket back to the circulation desk. As he checked in materials, he'd review the borrowers' names and try to figure out who might've inadvertently misplaced his filthy porno rag. *His*. Simon was confident that he was using the correct possessive pronoun under the circumstances. The publication of such periodicals was a blemish on the collective character of the male gender, and he'd have a word with the magazine's owner about basic decency if he could track him down.

Simon glanced at the clock that hung next to the portrait of Queen Elizabeth. It was 8:25. Plenty of time to search for clues before the other staff arrived. He noted the magazine was on the bottom of the pile, which meant it was first into the slot after 8:00 pm the previous evening, when the library closed for the night.

Simon set the magazine on the desk blotter and looked at the cover. February 2003. An old issue, but what would that matter to men who "read" such things? A blonde woman with full, luridly painted lips, her long hair covering her bare breasts, leered at him from the cover. Simon felt a tightening inside his pants. He had to pull his eyes away to search for more clues inside the magazine. As he turned over the cover page, he noticed a pink paper clip pinned at the top. Inside was a post-it note. Interesting, thought Simon. Adhesive and clip, like a belt and suspenders. Someone didn't want to lose the note. Then he read it. "Turn to the 'Penthouse Pet' in the centrefold." Simon did as the note commanded.

Pictured in a two-page spread was the blonde cover girl, as naked as Eve in the garden, her long limbs sprawled provocatively. Taped over the girl's face was a cut-out, passport-style photo of Grace. Immediately,

Simon felt sick to his stomach. Scrawled in black marker was a taunt. "The mole on the inside of your wife's thigh turns me on!" And oddly, perhaps intentionally, the dot on the exclamation point landed exactly on the top of the inner thigh of the Penthouse girl where Grace was marked with a real mole.

Simon abruptly closed the magazine and buried it under a stack of old files in the bottom drawer of the desk. He didn't want to share this unsettling discovery with an early bird colleague. Instead he turned to the basket and quickly looked for suspicious men among the borrowers as he checked the returns through the computer…

Dorothy Checketts: a boxed set of DVDs of the 'Midsomer Murders'

Gabrielle Tam: *Careers for Humanities Grads*, *What Colour is Your Parachute,* and three how-to books on resume writing

Harold Pincher: three CDs- *Waltzes and Polkas, Let's Celebrate with Strauss, and Wagner Unwound*

Olivia Southey: several paperbacks from the 'Babysitter Club' series

Madison Holman: two how-to books on knitting baby clothes, *Yoga for the Expectant Woman* in hard cover, and an array of magazines on parenting, crafting, and cookery

Alvin Wheeler: two westerns by Louis L'Amour and a *Dummies' Guide* to estate planning.

And that was it… a lighter than usual haul, and nary a miscreant among these patrons.

Simon remembered a recent staff meeting he'd attended. The oily maintenance fellow, Carsten, reported that repairs to the CCTV monitoring system would cost several hundred dollars. The librarians agreed to defer repairs in favour of acquiring materials. After all, they argued, what was the point of monitoring a building with bare shelves? Carsten shook his head and said they'd "rue the decision to neglect basic security." His words were prophetic.

On the other hand, Carsten knew the CCTV system was down, and Simon wouldn't put it past the man to read pornography… or steal another man's bride. Simon's chest puffed at the thought of defending Grace's honour, however dubious it might be. His obsession with uncovering the identity of his wife's secret lover began–for real–at 8:42.

▼▼▼

At 8:43, Margot pushed through the staff door and bumped her way to the circulation desk, her glasses foggy from leaving a cold November morning for the always-August, twenty-three degrees of the library interior. Simon muttered an impatient "good morning" to his colleague.

Margot was punctual, and she adored books, but she was otherwise unsuited to her duties. First, she was sloppy when the task at hand required accuracy. Just yesterday, Simon found a children's book on aviation in the adult's section, courtesy of — you guessed it — Margot. Furthermore, she deserted the circulation desk whenever a patron approached her with research query she found even passingly interesting.

And her wardrobe! Today she wore a tweed blazer over a burgundy cable-knit sweater over a plaid men's shirt with a canary-yellow infinity scarf encircling the whole pile of rags. Simon knew that Margot wouldn't deign to use the hook provided for outdoor clothing at the staff entrance. No, no, no. All morning, she'd discard items on chairbacks and desktops until she was down to the plaid shirt with its sleeves rumpled up to her elbows. Her unkempt appearance reflected her organizational skills and tested Simon's tolerance for difference. Worst of all? Margot didn't seem to care.

"Good morning, Simon," said Margot. She wiped her glasses on the hem of her shirt, which now protruded from under the waistband of the sweater. "Who's up for 'Tales for Tots' this morning?"

"It's your turn, Margot. If you refer to the schedule…" Simon gestured toward a photocopied calendar page pinned to the bulletin board with "Margot" highlighted in mauve on all four Thursdays.

"Cool," said Margot. "It's windy outside and the kids like making animal noises. I think I'll start with *Farmer Brown Goes Round and Round.*"

"A stimulating choice," said Simon. He expected an excessive rise in decibel level from the children's area by 10:05. "Perhaps something a little more… umm… sedate after *Farmer Brown*? Something soothing?"

"Wise," replied Margot. "I'll read the brats an article on tax law. That'll tranquilize them." She shook her head and sat on the desk, another annoying habit.

Simon set aside his irritation and asked, nonchalantly, "Have you found any… umm… unusual materials in the returns lately? Anything… perhaps… unsuitable?"

Margot leaned forward and stared over her glasses. "Such as what?"

"Well… umm… something smutty, perhaps. That shouldn't be in the library."

"If you ask me, Simon, the library needs more smut. Romances fly off the shelves and, let me tell you, they aren't your granny's Harlequins these days. If we want to serve our customers, we should have a whole section of erotica."

Customers. Simon shrugged the word away. Terminology such as 'customers' and 'users' commercialised the library and diminished the institution's noble goal of elevating the literary sensibilities of the citizens of Elmington.

"Let's revisit that idea at our next acquisitions meeting," said Simon. "I'm asking about items that belong in someone's private collection."

"Whose?"

"Never mind, Margot. By your answers, I'm given to believe that you, as usual, have no pertinent information to present."

"I suppose not," said Margot. She turned to the IT technician, who was hanging up his Gore-Tex parka. "Morning Colin. Simon is wondering if we've seen anything untoward in the library. Anything pornographic."

Colin sucked air through his teeth and gazed at the ceiling for a moment. "Well, as a matter of fact, I have."

"Do tell," said Margot.

"I caught old Harold Pincher watching porn on the catalogue computer a week ago Monday. I told him to take his fascination to the computer in the study area… to be discreet."

"And?" asked Margot.

"And he did. It was hetero, straight up, man on woman sex in the missionary position. Harmless but not something a mother wants to explain to a preschooler in the library. The end," replied Colin.

Simon was flustered. Harold Pincher? With Grace? Now Simon's main suspect was 85 years old, plus or minus a year, and travelled by taxi because he'd relinquished his licence. Colin should've reported this incident post-haste, but Simon decided to ignore his colleague's negligence. "Thank-you for the information, Colin," said Simon.

"No probs," said Colin.

"You're welcome," corrected Simon. He looked at the clock. It was almost nine.

▼▼▼

Simon crossed the threshold of his front door at approximately five pm. Usually, he looked forward to sliding into his slippers, perhaps changing into jeans and a sweatshirt, and relaxing with a beverage. His workday had passed unremarkably, but he was wound up like a Timex wristwatch. Tic, tic, tic. Unwinding would be impossible.

As he pushed a hanger into the sleeves of his overcoat, Simon was comforted, briefly, by the smell of roasting meat wafting from the kitchen, down the wall-papered corridor, to his nostrils.

"Simon? You're home?" Grace's voice broke Simon's brief reprieve.

He decided against replying. It was a husband's prerogative to be silent if he wished.

"Simon? Oh, there you are." Grace stood in the doorway to the kitchen, a paring knife glinting in her right hand.

Simon nodded.

"TGIT, Simon."

Simon raised a curious brow as Grace stepped toward him.

"Thank God It's Thursday." She kissed his stone-cold cheek. "Do you want a glass of wine to celebrate?"

Simon shrugged a non-committal 'yes' and took note of the music issuing from the radio. 'Ride of the Valkyries.' Harold Pincher had returned 'Wagner Unwound.' A coincidence? Simon thought not. He had to behave naturally if he hoped to discover the truth, so he broke his silence. "You usually listen to the news when you cook."

"Well, the news is all about that mass shooting yesterday and I can't bear it, so I switched to Radio 2." Grace poured Simon a glass of red wine and passed it to him.

"And you chose Wagner over The Tragically Hip or some other rock and roll music?"

"I suppose I'm growing up. Becoming more cultured

like you. Adulting."

Simon disliked Grace's penchant for turning nouns into verbs. She was too old for that cutesy linguistic affectation. He hid his irritation and asked, "Why Wagner? Why not jazz, or country?"

"Country? Are you off your rocker, Simon? What's the matter? You're acting weird."

"I'm not acting weirdly. I'm surprised you enjoy the same music as old men do, that's all." Simon sipped his wine and observed Grace's reaction.

"What?" Grace looked perplexed, but Simon thought she might be faking.

"Old men. Elderly, white octogenarians. Do you find them interesting? Or sexy?" asked Simon. "Some women do. Hugh Hefner attracted a harem of young women. And Harold Pincher has a roguish sense of style. He wears a fedora."

"Simon, I don't know why you're asking these crazy questions, but I assure you, I don't dig old dudes. And I'm pretty sure the Bunnies rolled in the grass at the Playboy mansion because Hugh paid them to do it." Grace set her wine glass on the counter and put her arms around Simon's neck. "You're all the man I want, and all the man I can handle."

Simon retreated to his usual pretense of contented husband-hood. He'd prepare thoroughly before questioning Grace again. He kissed his wife on the forehead and asked about supper.

▼▼▼

On Friday morning, Simon's heart beat like a metronome dialed up to a nervous *allegro* as he walked to the after-hours receptacle. However, Simon's trepidation soon gave way to relief. The returns were wholly uncontroversial and dull: two issues of *Conde Nast Traveler*; three tea cozy mysteries by M.C. Beaton; a stray bookmark with a rust-coloured tassel for the Capricorn reader; an assortment of children's picture books; *Veganism for Leather Lovers*; and a collection of short stories by Alice Munro, the most pornographic finding of the lot in Simon's estimation. He decided that Thursday had been an anomaly… a day to box up and forget.

Tranquility prevailed until midday when Simon witnessed an event that was at once prosaic and alarming. A female patron approached the circulation desk with a complaint about a computer monitor, a fussy piece of equipment that preferred to relay information upside-down despite Colin's frequent ministrations. Simon summoned Colin with a brisk tap on the bell at the IT workstation, and Colin arrived and received the complaint.

"Acting up again, is it?" Colin's eyes met the patron's with earnest concern. "Thank-you for letting me know. I hope you found another computer."

The patron told Colin she had.

"Good, good. I'll fix that monitor as soon as I can," Colin said gravely.

Then, Colin opened a drawer and removed a pad of post-it notes, took a Sharpie from the pen holder, and scribbled, "Out of order!"

Simon's marrow turned to ice. "That note…" he

said, pointing his index finger at the colored pad.

"Yes, I'll fix the naughty beast after lunch. For now, I want people to stay off that monitor or we'll be hearing about it constantly."

"But you wrote in marker and used an exclamation point when none was required."

"Oh, for God's sake, Simon. Your micromanaging is out of control."

Simon had to admit, he sounded ridiculous. Yet Colin's writing resembled the writing on the note in the magazine. Both messages were masculine, blocky, and sure handed. He'd compare the two samples later, when the coast was clear.

"Fair enough, Colin," said Simon, his tone conciliatory. "Why don't you take your break now, and I'll go when Margot's back."

"Alright, Simon," agreed Colin. He walked to the catalogue computers and, with a redundant, inch-long piece of tape, affixed the note to the troublesome monitor. Belt and suspenders—again.

▼▼▼

Alas, Simon had no chance to compare the notes due to heavy patron traffic by the circulation desk over the lunch hour. Colin adjusted the monitor during Simon's break and presumably disposed of the "out of order" sign. Simon checked every garbage can for a crumpled, yellow post-it note but found none. Highly irregular, thought Simon.

Margot and Colin accepted Simon's offer to leave at

4:30 pm, permitting Simon to wait alone for the evening librarian, the habitually tardy Bianca. He removed the *Penthouse* magazine from the bottom drawer and put it in the inside pocket of his overcoat, pausing in the task to peek at the note concealed under page one. The handwriting was similar, but not the same as Colin's. Perhaps Colin disguised his style when he scrawled the damning words implicating Grace in the sordid act of adultery. Simon needed more clues before he could confront his wife.

▼▼▼

It was Simon's turn to work solo on Saturday morning, a dreary November day. A persistent sleet pelted Elmington, weather that would chase people from the parks and streets into the armchairs of the library as soon as Simon unlocked the doors.

He opened the after-hours receptacle and found a hard-covered *National Geographic* atlas, three romance novels, a glorified comic book titled *Watchmen*, and several soft-covered European travel guides, likely returned by a single patron who'd exceeded borrowing limits. Margot! Smoke led to fire, and a violation of policy led to Margot every time. Simon imagined her at the circulation desk, laughing and asking the patron about his or her itinerary. If there were four books about Provence on the desk, she'd suggest a fifth, as if she were urging canapes on a guest at a cocktail party. Incorrigible!

Simon breathed his irritation away. He needn't ruminate about Margot's flagrant disregard for rules on a perfectly ordered Saturday. What's more, the inclement weather had dampened the exuberance of the Friday-night vandals and litterbugs, and the receptacle was devoid of garbage. Simon swept his arm through the box to confirm it was empty and pulled out a pamphlet.

What a pamphlet it was. On its face was a photograph of four partially clothed adults holding hands—two women, two men, four hues of the dermatological rainbow. Below the photo, a caption in inflammatory red lettering asked, impertinently, "Friend, is polyamory the answer?"

"The answer to what?" Simon asked back. Then he saw the paperclip. Pink as before, inviting him to open the pamphlet. Inside, a post-it note covered the top of one of three panels of clumsily typeset paragraphs on the merits of multiple-partner romance. Rendered in a blocky, masculine hand with black marker was the message, "Information for Simon Woodburn".

Simon blushed. Although his red face suggested otherwise, Simon was no hothouse tomato. He was a well-educated, open-minded man… and aware of societal trends. Why would anyone want to give him an instructive pamphlet on polyamory?

Simon lugged his basket to the circulation desk and hid the pamphlet in his overcoat pocket. He decided to investigate the borrowing patterns of certain persons of interest. He had thirty minutes till opening. He logged into the computer.

A five second foray into Colin's digital record revealed a single download onto a Kobo e-reader on December 23rd, the mark of a semi-literate IT professional personalizing a gift for his mother. Colin's borrowing history was otherwise blank.

Carsten had borrowed books on vintage motorcycles and sports cars, several Jack Reacher novels, and every classic rock CD in the library's collection, an unremarkable history congruent with Simon's expectations of a middle-aged maintenance worker. Simon didn't bother checking Harold Pincher's history. In retrospect, the odds of Harold seducing Grace were remote.

Simon locked his fingers together and stretched his arms over his head to reset his brain. There were more ways than one to skin a cat or snoop. Perhaps he'd approached the problem backward. He typed 'polyamory' into the query field of the catalogue. Ten items appeared: six books; three e-books; and one large print book. Simon clicked on *More Than Two: An Ethical Guide to Polyamory.* The item was checked out, on loan to Sylvia Johnson. Simon gasped. The next name on the list was Grace Woodburn.

Simon dove into Grace's borrowing history as fast as his finger could click the mouse. *Opening Up: A Guide to Creating and Sustaining Open Relationships* and *The Polyamorists Next Door* and *Redefining our Relationships*... all three had been borrowed in October by Grace Angelica Woodburn, his bride, his true love, his soulmate. She must've known he'd find the list. Grace's borrowing history was a cry for help, a drowning sex addict's plea for a life-preserver. Simon could think of no other explanation for Grace's interest in books on polyamory. Worse, someone sinister, someone who meant to steal Grace, was tossing her a line.

Simon looked at the clock. 8:50. He pressed numbers into the phone, urgently, authoritatively. Bianca answered on the fourth ring with a groggy, "Hello?"

"Hello, Bianca? It's Simon," he said. "I've been called to an emergency… a member of my family. I must leave the library as soon as possible."

Bianca agreed to receive the baton within the hour. He'd open the great oak doors and gather books and puppets for the story-time volunteer, and then, as soon as Bianca arrived, he'd rescue Grace from her terrible loneliness as the wife of a duty-bound head librarian who worked every third weekend.

▼▼▼

Simon bounded up the walkway, unlocked the front door, burst into the hall, and tripped over a pair of Blundstones. Simon examined the scuffed boots from floor level. They looked familiar, but they weren't Grace's. He picked himself up and stood, still as a hunter listening at forest's edge. The bungalow was silent. Or was it?

Simon heard a giggle, high-pitched, muffled under blankets, a sound from boyhood, from the time his sister held a slumber party. Again, the house was silent. Simon walked through the living room toward the master bedroom. He heard another giggle.

A weak light flooded the carpet from the east window of the bedroom. Simon deduced the door was open. He rounded the jamb and crept across the hooked rug beside the bed. Tendrils of auburn hair spilled over the pillow. Grace was hidden under the duvet, her form oddly large and lumpy. The giggle rose to laughter.

A voice, husky with mirth, said, "Hello, Simon. Care to join us?" A familiar hand decorated with chipped blue nail polish and silver rings and bangles emerged and pushed the duvet down.

"Margot?"

"Present," said Margot.

"Grace!"

"Also present," said Margot.

The two women were locked in an embrace that was not at all sisterly and not at all chaste. Immediately Simon felt disconnected from planet earth. His mind raced of its own volition toward a strange, unworldly destination. As a librarian, he was accustomed to finding answers, using language, specifically English, and although he wasn't sure if any language would be helpful, he had no other tool at hand for cleaving onto reality.

"You're lovers?" Simon asked.

"Correct," replied Margot.

"If you don't mind, I'd prefer it if Grace answered the questions," said Simon.

Margot nodded, and Grace said, "Okay. Yes, Simon, as you can see, we're having sex."

The Indelicacy of Grace's reply shocked Simon. "How long have you been… umm… dating?" he asked.

"Since last summer," replied Grace.

"Did you know about the *Penthouse* magazine, Grace?"

"Yes. It was Margot's idea. She thought it was playful. She said it'd get you excited. Intrigued."

“Get your motor running…” sang Margot.

“Be quiet, Margot,” said Simon. Scolding her felt invigorating. “And the pamphlet?”

“That was my idea,” said Grace. “But the post-it notes… that was pure Margot. She’s so creative.”

Simon paused his interrogation and surveyed the matrimonial bedroom, now sullied with another woman’s woolen knitwear, denim, and intimate apparel. Tears pooled in his eyes.

“Simon?” Grace sat on the side of the bed and took his hand. “Simon? Is it so awful as that?”

Simon didn’t answer. He turned from Grace, leaned over the dresser, and regarded his sad face in the mirror. It was the face of a man betrayed, but not at all bad looking. In fact, Simon thought himself rather handsome in his misery. Intelligent of brow, and brave of jaw.

“Simon? Would you consider a new arrangement? In our household?”

Simon squared his shoulders. “I don’t know, Grace. I’m going for a walk. And Margot? Please be gone by the time I’m back. Grace and I have matters to discuss. As husband and wife.”

The scales had fallen from Simon’s eyes, and he was taking charge.

Renee Lehnen

Renee Lehnen is a registered nurse who works in a long-term care home. Due to shift work, she often writes when most people are sleeping, and her favourite subjects are neurosis, illness, and death. Recently, her satirical novel, Elmington, was awarded "Best Unpublished Manuscript" of 2022 by Crime Writers of Canada. Before discovering the vibrant world of creative writing, she completed a bachelor's degree in environmental studies and a master's degree in history.

Renee lives in Stratford, Ontario, Canada with her husband who is also a nurse.

Eugene Angove and the Perilous Peregrination

Tim Mendees

January 7th, 1939:

Holding his breath, Doctor Jason Blackburn quietly opened the door to his sleeper compartment and slipped out into the corridor. The rectangular shafts of light cast by the gibbous moon gave the darkened passage an almost abstract beauty. After checking that his assistant, Ruby Radcliff, was sleeping soundly, he pulled the door gently closed. Stifling the *click* of the latch with his gloved palm, Jason finally exhaled. His pulse was racing... he loved this part.

The LNER's flagship locomotive, The Flying Scotsman rattled and shook as it crossed the rolling hills and valleys of lowlands Scotland. Jason's furtive eyes darted left and right as he checked that he was alone. Satisfied, he put on his shoes and crept down the corridor. He winced slightly with every silent step. In not wanting to risk waking Ruby, he had stood on her hatpin with his stockinged foot. The fact that he did not yelp with pain was a testament to the man's grit.

Tiptoeing past all the other compartments, he listened for any activity. As he had planned, the other passengers appeared to have either gone down to the dining carriage for supper at midnight or were getting spruced up in the WCs beforehand. Feigning illness so he and his assistant could *retire* without scrutiny had been a stroke of genius. The salacious tongues of the other passengers had been wagging ever since they had arrived at the archaeological dig in the woods near Gabhar Vale. Every man and woman on board was aware that his and Ruby's relationship was not purely professional. They were guaranteed to believe that their withdrawal was simply a gossamer-thin ruse to sneak in a bit of clandestine rumpy-pumpy. Jason smiled. There would be time for that later. Right now, he had a job to do.

Jason felt a slight pang of guilt as he pulled open the door at the end of the corridor and stepped out into the night. He did not particularly like deceiving Ruby. But needs must when the Devil drives. The icy Scottish wind bit at his ears as he passed between carriages and slipped into another sleeper car. Nobody was allocated to this one, so he relaxed. Aside from the eight other passengers, there was only the driver, stoker, a cook, a waiter, and a guard on board. And they were all down the opposite end of the train. He was anticipating plain sailing from that point onwards.

Quickening his pace, Blackburn made his way past the compartments, pausing briefly to mop his brow with a monogrammed handkerchief. Despite the cold, he was sweating profusely. Adrenaline always had that effect on him. He could taste its metallic sharpness in the back of his throat. He was going to need a stiff drink or three once the deed was done. Upon leaving the carriage, he skipped over to the baggage car with renewed vigour. His task was almost complete.

Lighting the oil lamp that hung on a nail by the door with a *Swan Vestas* match, he illuminated the cluttered compartment. The eggy smell of sulphur mingled noxiously with the musty aroma of things long buried. Crates containing stones covered in strange carvings and bizarre pictographs were piled high against the scratch wooden panelling. While the rest of the train was salubrious, this car would have been much more at home coupled to a freight locomotive. Clearly, the fastidious cleaning regime only reached those parts of the train open for passengers.

"Where are you, you little beauty?" Blackburn purred, stroking his pencil moustache with a thumb and forefinger. Sweeping the lamp left and right, he looked for a crate that he had covertly marked with a series of notches around the lid. He had been careful to make them look like the marks a crowbar would leave, but he would know them anywhere.

"Ah!" He exclaimed in triumph, spotting the crate over in the far corner. "There you are you cheeky little minx."

Stepping over piles of camping and digging equipment, Jason clambered over to the crate and placed the lamp on the ground. Looking around, he spotted a crowbar leaning against a selection of grubby shovels. Slipping the flat end under the lid and putting his weight on the other end, he prised the lid open just enough to slip his hand inside. He had packed the crate and had ensured that what he desired was right at the top. Grinning to himself, he pulled out the cold stone artefact and slipped it into his pocket.

"Got you..." He smirked, unaware that while he had been busy, someone had come silently into the carriage behind him. As he removed the crowbar and began to replace the lid, a shadowy figure walked up behind him, arm raised.

Thunk!

A heavy object was brought down with brutal efficiency on the back of Jason Blackburn's cranium. The force of the blow split his skull and dropped him like a sack of spuds. He fell forwards with his head striking the floor next to the lamp. His prolonged death rattle extinguished the flame and plunged the carriage into darkness...

▼▼▼

Eugene Angove's bushy eyebrows knitted together as he tried to stab a pea with his fork. The sway of the train had the small green vegetable rolling back and forth on his plate. In the end, it all became too much, and he squashed it flat in a fit of pique. "Bloody peas... who in their right mind decides to serve peas on a moving train?"

His faithful valet, Hampton, smirked as he poured his employer another glass of *vin rouge*. "Perhaps the cook is a sadist, sir." He chuckled.

"You know, Hampton, old chap. That wouldn't surprise me one little bit on this trip." Eugene gestured to the rest of the dining cart. "I've never met such a rum bunch."

Hampton looked around discreetly. Eugene was not joking. At the far end of the room were a red-faced military man and his valet. Next to them was a rotund elderly nun chatting with an enormous Sikh. Finally, sitting alone with a table covered in notes and maps was the refined Professor Mirabelle. Conspicuous by their absence were Doctor Blackburn and his glamorous assistant, Ruby Radcliff. "It certainly is a motley collection for an archaeological team, Sir... I must say, I'm surprised that you agreed to get mixed up in all of this."

Eugene shovelled a dollop of mashed potato and horseradish sauce into his maw and chewed. He let his fork *clatter* to his plate and tapped his bulbous nose with a pudgy forefinger. "I have my reasons, Hampton." He said at last. "Let's just say that Miss Stephenson made me an offer I couldn't refuse."

"Ahh." Hampton nodded sagely. He could tell by the glint in his employer's eye that vast sums of cash or something he could sell for vast sums of cash was behind his enthusiasm. Normally, Eugene would not touch anything to do with the Brotherhood of Tamesis with a ten-foot pole... not after all the fuss over the Black Stone of Tsathoggua. It probably helped that Edith Stephenson recruited him and not her adoptive sibling. He would have told Algernon to go and whistle...

"After all, it's a simple enough job." Eugene continued, sloshing more wine into his glass. "Escort a bunch of academics, religious types, and some buffoon from the Army, up to the back end of beyond and keep an eye on them while they escort some kind of Pagan bauble back down to London. Once it's safely in the vault of the British Museum, job done." He paused to lean in conspiratorially. "Between you and me, Hampton. I was treating this trip as an opportunity to sample some of the local whiskey!"

Hampton rolled his eyes as Eugene roared with laughter. He certainly took advantage of that opportunity. On the first night in Gabhar Vale, Eugene had guzzled so much of the local tipple that he had ended up having to be carted back to his tent in a rusty wheelbarrow. He had been worse than useless for the next two days, forcing Hampton to do all of the keeping an eye on things. Eugene just lay on his bedroll, groaning and complaining about the profusion of midges.

"Well," Eugene smirked. "The item in question is safely on board the train... I can't see how anything can go wrong now... No, for once, I think this is easy money. "

As Hampton opened his mouth to tell Eugene not to jinx things, the door at the far end of the carriage burst open, startling the nun. It was Ruby Radcliff. She was white as a sheet and visibly shaken. "Come quickly!" She shrieked. "Doctor Blackburn has been murdered!"

▼▼▼

"Well, Hampton... that'll teach me to keep my ruddy trap shut." Eugene shook his head as he looked down at Blackburn's rapidly cooling corpse. "What's the verdict, then?"

"Well," Hampton sniffed as he examined the wound to the back of the late doctor's head. "There are no ligature marks or signs of gunshot or stab wounds. The only wound I can see is this big dent in the back of his head. It's a savage blow. I'd say it killed him almost instantly."

"Any idea what the murder weapon could be?"

"Well, judging by the shape of the wound... a candlestick, maybe?"

"On a train? Don't be daft, Hampton."

Hampton frowned at Eugene. "It could be any blunt object. A lead pipe or a spanner, perhaps. Look around, Sir." He gestured to the myriad shovels, picks, and other tools. "Take your pick... no pun intended."

"What the blazes are you two wittering on about like a pair of old washerwomen?" The military man, Colonel Tewksbury, climbed over the equipment to join Eugene and Hampton. He had been at the far end of the carriage barking orders at his valet, Dwight LeBlanc. The Sikh, Arju, and Professor Mirabelle were in the opposite corner, looking on silently. Sister Olive had stayed in the dining car to look after Ruby.

"The poor chap's had his head caved in," Eugene stated flatly. "From the looks of things, he was trying to pinch something from this crate, and someone clobbered him from behind.

“We’d better search the train then.” Tewksbury puffed out his chest. “The murderer can’t have gone far...”

Eugene looked pointedly at the other guests, then the Colonel. “No... he or she couldn’t.”

“What are you implying?” Tewksbury barked, his moustache bristling.

“Well, Hampton and I did a thorough search of the train when we left Edinborough. Aside from a few staff, there is only us lot on board, so...” He shrugged and let his words hang heavy in the air.”

“But” Tewksbury argued. “We were all in the dining car, surely.”

Hampton looked up from his squatted position. “We don’t know exactly when it happened... it could have been any time between him going to bed with Miss Radcliff and us getting here.”

“Hampton’s right,” Eugene added, producing his hip flask from his inside pocket. “We will have to appraise ourselves with everybody’s movements. I suggest you all return to the dining car, and we will be along presently.”

“Look here, Angove...” Tewksbury growled. “I represent His Majesty’s Army... I’m in charge. I will not take orders from a drunken *adventurer*.” He let the final word ooze with disdain. Eugene had been a Captain during the Great War but had long since been a civilian. He was not going to be taking orders either. The two men had been butting heads ever since they clapped eyes on each other. Hampton saw them as two over-the-hill stags locking horns.

“And you look *here*.” Eugene grinned, taking an

official document signed by Edith Stephenson and Neville Chamberlain from his blazer and tapping it with his finger. "I think you'll find that both the Brotherhood of Tamesis *and* the Prime Minister have put *me* in charge... *Colonel.*"

Hampton turned his attention back to Blackburn's corpse, desperately trying not to snigger. If it was a competition in condescension that Tewksbury wanted... he was fixing to be outclassed. Nobody could top Eugene when it came to being patronising and obnoxious.

Tewksbury was fuming. His cheeks flushed red as he turned sharply and marched back towards the door. "Come along, LeBlanc!" He barked, as though the slight fellow was a green private, not an ageing valet. "I can tell when I'm not wanted."

"Very good Colonel," LeBlanc simpered, holding the door for Tewksbury.

Once they had left, slamming the door behind them, Eugene chuckled to himself. "That Tewksbury fellow really is a charmless blister, don't you agree, Hampton?"

Hampton raised a finger.

"I know... I know... The code forbids you speaking out of turn about your betters." Eugene smirked. "Fine... don't talk. Nod once for yes and twice for no."

Hampton nodded.

"Professor Mirabelle?" Eugene called out as she and Arju turned to leave.

"Yes, what is it, Angove?"

"Could you come over here and check that nothing is missing from this crate? You may as well go back to the dining car, Arju."

Arju nodded curtly and left.

"Um... Why, yes... I suppose." Mirabelle arced an immaculately plucked eyebrow over her wire-rimmed spectacles. "What about... him?" She pointed at the corpse with a tremulous digit.

"He's not going to cause you any bother, Professor... surely, you're not squeamish?"

"Well," Mirabelle shrugged, her gut-glass voice wavering. "It's just that I've never seen a dead body before."

"Ha!" Eugene erupted. "Did you hear that, Hampton? The woman that spends her life digging up skulls and cataloguing bones has never dealt with a dead body before."

"Yes, but they don't have *meat* on them."

Eugene chuckled, then had a gulp of brandy.

"It's alright, Professor. I've finished gathering his personal effects." Hampton added, helpfully. "If you could pass me that tarpaulin over yonder, I can cover him up for you."

"Thank you, Hampton," Mirabelle said as she passed over the bundle. "At least one of you is a gentleman."

Her cutting remark merely made Eugene chuckle even louder. "They don't have meat on them... priceless!"

"Oh, out of the way, you big oaf!" Once Blackburn had been covered, Mirabelle elbowed Eugene out of the way and picked up the crowbar. For one minute, Hampton thought she was going to brain Eugene with it. She did not. Instead, she levered up the lid then started to rummage in the crate.

“What did you find on the late lamented, Hampton?” Eugene asked, finally pulling himself together.

“Not much, Sir. Just some travel papers, a cigarette case, a packet of matches, and a monogrammed handkerchief.” Hampton passed the documents to Eugene. “Wait... that’s odd.”

“What is?” Eugene unfolded the documents and started to examine them.

“Well... this handkerchief, Sir. It’s monogrammed, JS. Not JB.”

Eugene waved this off. “He probably bought the wrong ones... he didn’t strike me as the sharpest knife in the draw. Despite all of his fancy qualifications.”

“True, Sir. But the cigarette case is also engraved, JS.”

“Hmm.” Eugene’s brow creased. “These documents appear to have been faked, also. You see this squiggle down here?” He pointed to one of the signatures. “This is supposed to be our old chum Stephenson’s mark... it’s no such thing. It doesn’t even look vaguely similar.”

“Cripes! Sir, you are right!” Hampton exclaimed. “But... it managed to fool the bluebottles at St Pancras!”

“Yes, well... I have long since said that the British Transport Police haven’t got a single brain cell amongst the lot of them.” Eugene paused for a moment. “So... If our stiff here isn’t the redoubtable Doctor Blackburn. Then who the bally hell is he?”

Hampton shrugged.

“Blast it! … There goes my thoughts of a nice relaxing journey. We need to get to the bottom of this... or Edith will have me stuffed and mounted before you could say, *Sherlock Holmes!*"

"It gets worse." Professor Mirabelle added in dire tomes.

"What is it, Professor?"

She turned to Eugene with wide eyes. "The amulet of Shub-Niggurath... it's gone!"

▼▼▼

"What's so important about this trinket then, Professor?" Eugene asked as they made their way through the vacant sleeper car. All the compartment doors were now open, and the rooms appeared to have been searched.

Professor Mirabelle sighed. "The amulet of Shub-Niggurath is said to be a powerful talisman... when used in conjunction with certain passages in *The Necronomicon*, it is said to..."

"Say no more." Eugene held his hand up. "Anything even vaguely connected with *that* book can't be good."

"It's not. When a couple of hikers stumbled across what turned out to be the ruins of a shrine to the Black Goat of the Woods With a Thousand Young, the BOT contacted me to search for anything *dangerous.*"

"Why you?"

"Because, Mr Angove, I am one of Britain's leading experts on the Great Old Ones."

"Well, Hampton. That explains why we are here... Edith could have warned us."

"You mean, you didn't know *what* we were transporting?" Mirabelle was incredulous.

Hampton cut in before Eugene could answer. "Mr

Angove didn't attend the briefing at The Mitre. I'm afraid he was... *indisposed*."

Now it was Professor Mirabelle's time to roar with laughter. "Oh, bravo, Hampton. Delicately put... I'm assuming by, *indisposed* you mean, as drunk as a newt?"

Both men flushed. One with embarrassment. The other with mirth.

"Well, to sum up, Mr Angove. The Amulet of Shub-Niggurath mustn't fall into the wrong hands... least of all those brown-shirted swines from Deutschland. You do know that Herr Himmler is trying to get his grubby mitts on as many occult items as he possibly can?"

"The Spook Brigade, you mean?"

"Yes, Der Ahnenerbe... The SS Occult Division. Well, our spies told us that they had gotten wind of the amulet and that Himmler prized it dearly... hence the motley crew we have here today.

Eugene nodded. "I understand. It all makes a bit more sense now. I was wondering why we had a Colonel on board. And, I'm assuming that the nun is here for a bit of divine intervention should things go wrong?"

Mirabelle shrugged. "I suppose so. I confess to not knowing much about our companions. Aside from Arju, that is."

"Ah, yes. The big chap. Who is he anyway?"

"He's my assistant, on loan from Oxford. We met on a dig in New Delhi. We were out there looking for the Temple of Yig. He proved to be a useful asset when things got a little *rough.* So, when this came up, I head-hunted him. He's terribly knowledgeable about the Old Ones..."

"And built like a brick outhouse." Eugene smiled.

"Quite."

Hampton nipped ahead and opened the doors to the next carriage for them. It seemed that there was some kind of ruckus going on down the far end. "Um... Sir? I think we may have trouble brewing."

After letting Professor Mirabelle go first, he stepped into the carriage and surveyed the scene. Arju and Colonel Tewksbury were standing chest to chest, hurling abuse at each other. "What the bloody hell is going on now?" Eugene bellowed.

"This *kuta* wants to ransack my room!" Arju answered, not taking his eyes off Tewksbury.

Mirabelle looked in her own compartment and found that it looked like a bomb had hit it. The bedding had been tossed, and all the storage spaces emptied. "What the devil do you think you are doing, Man?" Her notes and stationery were strewn across the floor.

Tewksbury puffed out his chest. "I'm searching for the intruder!"

"He's been in our room too, sir," Hampton muttered. Annoyingly, Tewksbury had rumpled tomorrow's shirts that he had laid out flat on the beds. "He's made a right old mess."

"What the buggery are you playing at, Tewksbury?" Eugene exploded. "If you've smashed my bottles of single malt, I will not be amused."

"Somebody had to do something aside from stand around yapping... and I would remind you that I am a colonel!" Whether it was a conscious thing for effect or not, the man snapped to attention. "I was conducting a room-by-room search. Look..." He moved away from Arju and opened the adjacent room. "I've even searched my room."

Eugene peered around the door and saw that it was in the same state as the others. "That's all well and good, but why the Dickens have you pulled all of the luggage out? Surely you don't think someone could be hiding in the overhead compartment. Who are you looking for... a blasted pixie?"

"My point exactly, Mr Angove." Arju nodded. "He can see that there is nobody in there. I just don't want him going through my things. He's tipped out the contents of my suitcase... look!"

"That was an accident."

"Accident or not. I don't want your grubby paws all over my clothes!" Arju folded his arms over his muscular chest.

Tewksbury went to argue but was silenced by a sibilant, "hush" from Professor Mirabelle. "Let us all just calm down, shall we? Are you satisfied that nobody is hiding in any of the compartments?"

Tewksbury sniffed. "I suppose."

"Right. Shall we all go through to the dining car, then? I'm sure you could do with a brandy, Colonel?"

"Well... erm... A wee snifter wouldn't go amiss."

"Come along then..." Mirabelle threaded her arm through his and steered him out of the carriage. Arju followed along after them, his eyes burning holes in Tewksbury's back.

Eugene was impressed. Professor Mirabelle had handled the situation deftly. Part mother, part headmistress.

Whatever she did, it worked. He made a mental note to try her approach in the future. Though, what the Colonel would think about linking arms with him was anybody's guess. Deciding that brandy was a fine idea, he took a nip from his flask before looking around in confusion. "Hampton? Where the devil have you got to?"

"In here, sir," Hampton called from the compartment adjacent to their own.

Eugene wandered over and peered through the door. Hampton was on his knees riffling through Doctor Blackburn's valise. "Find anything?"

"Not as yet... wait." Hampton upended the bag and tipped the contents onto the floor. Next, he produced his trusty butterfly knife and swung it open. It was an incongruous item for one so refined looking. The valet carried it for self-defence.

"What is it?"

There appears to be something sewn into the lining, Sir." With a *rip*, Hampton slit the fabric and reached inside. "Well, I'll be blown, Sir. Look... a German passport!"

"Ruddy hell!" Eugene whistled as he snatched the passport from Hampton's hands. "Say hello to Doctor Jayson Schwarz!"

"It gets worse, Sir... Look. It appears that our imposter was a member of the Schutzstaffel!" Hampton held up an SS ID card.

"Bugger me. Well, Mirabelle did say that Herr Himmler was interested in the amulet. He was obviously sent to pinch it... the sneaky bounder."

"Indeed, Sir. But, if he was the thief, where is it

now?"

"I don't know yet, Hampton, but I intend to find out. Come on, let's speak to our suspects..."

"How dare you suspect me of murder." Sister Olive fumed. Her thick Scottish accent rumbled from her larynx. She sounded like she was gargling jelly. "It's one of the Ten Commandments... Thou shalt not kill!" She stared unblinking at Eugene with her bulbous eyes. Her cold gaze made him shiver. She licked her wide fleshy lips before taking a deep breath.

Eugene quickly held his hand up, halting the incoming sermon. "I'm sorry, Sister. But I must ask everybody. You've just watched me ask everyone else the exact same question... what were your movements before you came for supper."

"Of all the nerve... *Movements* indeed."

"Sister. Please." Eugene held his hands up in supplication.

"Fine... if you must know. I was in the water closet... Travel makes me... *irregular*." The corpulent nun blushed. "Happy?" And, with that, she stood up and stormed out of the dining car in the direction of the kitchen and standard carriages.

Eugene looked at Hampton. "Well, as alibi's go... it's hardly cast-iron. When I asked about *movements,* I didn't mean..."

Hampton sniggered, despite himself. "Her reaction was a bit fishy, sir."

"Hmm." Eugene stroked his chin. "*Fishy* is one word for her..."

"Good lord!" Hampton piped, leaning in so nobody could overhear. "You don't think she's an Innsmouther, do you?"

"I'm afraid I do, Hampton. She definitely has *the look*. In any case, we need to find out one way or another."

"How do we do that, sir?"

"You need to get a look under her habit... see if she has gills."

"What?" Hampton yelped.

"Keep your bloody voice down."

"How the hell am I supposed to get her to remove her habit?"

"I don't know, Hampton." Eugene mused. "You're a resourceful chap. You'll think of something... Go on, off you toddle. I'm going to speak to Miss Radcliff. She has gone for a lie-down. So far, she's the most likely suspect. It was her that found the body, after all. And she has yet to explain what *she* was doing in the baggage car. Surely, she would have come here first if she was looking for Schwarz? I'm not buying her *'I went the wrong way'* explanation for a second."

"Fine." Hampton sighed. "Meet back here, sir?"

"Indeed, Hampton. Now, you have *duties* to attend to." Eugene patted his valet on the shoulder and grinned widely. "Good luck, old chap."

Hampton watched his employer depart. "And you, sir... with knobs on."

▼▼▼

Eugene steadied himself with a hand on the cold metal safety rail as the train rocked as it banked sharply to the left. Pulling the door to the sleeper car open, he hurried inside. Passing the WC, the portly adventurer nearly jumped out of his tweeds as the door flew open, revealing the ashen face of Dwight LeBlanc.

"Blimey, LeBlanc. You nearly gave me a sodding heart attack."

"Apologies, sir," LeBlanc answered as he dabbed his lips with a crumpled handkerchief. The man was looking decidedly green around the gills. There was a distinct puffiness to his pinched features.

Eugene's nose wrinkled as the pungent aroma of regurgitated sausage and mash drifted from the valet's gullet. "Everything alright?"

"Um... what? Err, yes, quite alright, Sir..." LeBlanc stammered, his eyes darting from left to right. "I'm afraid that I don't travel well. Now, if you will excuse me..."

"Yes, run along," Eugene said quietly as the furtive manservant scuttled out of the car like a whippet with a bee up its backside. "I wonder what the devil has put the wind up him?" With a shrug of his broad shoulders, Eugene turned and walked towards Miss Radcliff's compartment. She and the duplicitous Doctor Schwarz were in the compartment to the far side of his own. Eugene had to fight the urge to pop into his own room and have a nip of his treasured whiskey.

Reaching Ruby's door, he wrapped on it with his knuckle. "Miss Radcliff, may I come in? I have a few more questions I'd like to ask if I may?"

No answer.

Assuming that the distraught personal assistant was either sleeping or ignoring him, he knocked again. Louder this time. "Miss Radcliff... It really is a matter of the utmost importance."

Again, there was no answer.

"Oh, bugger this for a game of soldiers," Eugene grumbled. "Right! I'm coming in. If you are undressed, you might want to cover your bits and bobs!" With a *click,* he opened the door and instantly recoiled.

Ruby Radcliff was lying half on her bed, half off. As though she had been dragged off by her hair. A dagger had been plunged into her chest. From the positioning of the incision, it was pointless to check for a pulse. Eugene stepped into the room and checked the scene. Nothing else appeared to have changed since he and Hampton were in their earlier.

"Poor woman." Eugene sighed as he leaned over her corpse to examine the dagger. "Hold on... This is Professor Mirabelle's..." Mopping his brow with his sleeve, he turned and exited the compartment. "She has some explaining to do."

Hurrying through the carriage, Eugene made his way back to the dining car. Professor Mirabelle was still sitting where he had last seen her. Over by the window, scribbling in a notebook. She looked up as Eugene entered and one look at his expression told her that something was amiss.

"Is everything alright, Mr Angove? … How's Ruby."

"Dead as a bloody stone!" Eugene did not bother

softening the blow. He wanted to gauge her reaction.

"What?" Shocked, Mirabelle rose from her seat, clutching her chest. "What do you mean?"

"I mean, *dead*, Professor. As in, not breathing. Expired. Passed on. Pushing up the blasted daisies! What the Dickens do you think I mean?"

"But... how?"

"She's been stabbed..." Eugene paused for effect. "With y*our* dagger. That Indian one that you keep for *protection*."

"My dagger?" Mirabelle was aghast. If she did have something to do with it, she was a damn good actor. "How did someone get their hands on *my* dagger?" Suddenly, Eugene's implication became clear. "Wait... you can't possibly think?"

Eugene shrugged. "Did you?"

"Now look here, you blustering buffoon. How could I possibly have killed her? When she left, I was sitting here. You and Hampton were between me and the door. You would have seen me leave. Or are you so drunk that you forgot that small detail?"

"Well... erm..."

"*Hercule Poirot*, you most certainly are not... Pull yourself together, man!" Mirabelle snapped. "The real killer is still on the loose!"

"LeBlanc!" Eugene exclaimed, startling the Professor.

"I beg your pardon?"

"Where's LeBlanc... the colonel's valet?"

"He went that way." Mirabelle pointed to the opposite end of the carriage. "He didn't look at all well... you don't think?"

Eugene turned sharply while simultaneously patting his jacket for the comforting weight of his service revolver. Leaving Mirabelle to fuss with her papers, he strode off confidently. After all, Dwight LeBlanc was in his sixties and eight-stone when soaking wet. What possible trouble could he be if he turned nasty? Reaching out for the handle, he was nearly hit in the face by the door.

"There you are, sir," Hampton grumbled. He was rubbing his jaw, and his cheek was visibly red.

"What the hell happened to you?"

"Well, Sir. Let's just say, Sister Olive didn't appreciate me tipping a jug of water over her then trying to remove her habit so I could dry it... not one little bit." He worked his jaw up and down to check that it was not dislocated.

Eugene could not help chuckling. "Did you find anything out?"

"Indeed, Sir. She is *not* an Innsmouther... no gills. She does, however, have one hell of a right hook on her. If it came down to a championship bout with Len Harvey... my money would be on Sister Olive. The blasted woman's vicious!"

"Well done, anyway, dear fellow. You have helped narrow it down even further... For now, though, we need to have a little chat with Mr LeBlanc."

"Oh?"

Eugene proceeded to explain the recent developments to his personal gentleman. Hampton was particularly upset about Miss Radcliff's untimely demise. Judging her to be a true innocent in the whole affair... and a dashed nice girl to boot. First, she had been seduced by a German spy then slaughtered in cold blood by a Canadian valet... It was simply out of order.

"I'll give him a damn good thrashing, you see, if I don't." Hampton raged as they crossed into the carriage containing the kitchen and stores.

The galley was empty and in disarray. Eugene had told all the staff to remain in the guard carriage until the amulet had been recovered. Dirty crockery was piled in metal baskets awaiting the touch of soapy water. "Well, where the ruddy hell is he then?" Eugene bellowed, placing his hands on his hips."

"Standard class, perhaps... I didn't see him on the way through, Sir."

"Maybe he passed you when you were *otherwise engaged* with Sister Olive."

"Perhaps." Hampton rubbed his jaw again. It still stung like hell.

Passing the range and food preparation areas, Eugene and Hampton hurried towards the next door. As they reached the storage area, the train rocked as it took a sharp bend. There was a heavy *thump* against the door of the storage locker. Both men paused. Eugene drew his revolver instinctively. Putting his finger to his lips, he backed away and took aim. Giving Hampton the nod, he prepared to fire.

Hampton reached out and pulled the lever to open the door. It creaked as it swung open as the dead weight of Dwight LeBlanc fell against it. "Blimey, Sir! He's been garrotted!"

"Good Lord!" Eugene pocketed his firearm and

knelt. The murderer had used so much force that the ligature had bitten into the skin, drawing rivers of crimson that had stained the starched white collar of his shirt. "So much for him being our killer then."

"Indeed, sir." Hampton turned the man's head to get a look at the garotte. "Hold on. This is unusual."

"What... the rope? How interesting can a bally rope be, Hampton?"

"Very... if you know what you are looking for."

"Smugness doesn't suit you, Hampton." Eugene huffed.

"Apologies, Sir... It's just that this isn't ordinary rope. It's not made from hemp or cotton. It appears to be braided Indian silk..."

"Indian silk... Arju!" Eugene yelped in triumph. "Come along, Hampton... and bring that spanner with you. He's a big lad!"

Hampton looked around and saw what Eugene had indicated. He picked up the large adjustable spanner and followed on behind. "I don't understand it, Sir. The Sikh's are an honourable bunch. This kind of cloak and dagger business is anathema to them."

"That's if he is a Sikh, Hampton. Need I remind you that the garotte is the favoured weapon of the Thugee?"

"Point taken, Sir." Hampton shuddered. He and Eugene had spent some time in India after the war, and he had seen first-hand the handiwork of those notorious bandits.

Hampton led the way as they crashed into the first standard class carriage. Sister Olive was presently perched in a seat to the centre, knitting furiously.

Hampton›s pace quickened ever so slightly as he passed. The former regimental boxing champion knew when he was outmatched.

"Stay in your seat, Sister." Eugene bellowed, nearly making the nun drop what looked like a woollen nightmare into her lap. "There's a maniac on board."

She tutted then glared after Hampton. "How right you are!"

The two men crossed to the next carriage, with Hampton opening the door for Eugene. He stepped inside and drew his revolver. "Arju, halt!"

Arju was standing over Colonel Tewksbury brandishing a length of lead piping. The military man was on his knees, clutching his shoulder in pain. Arju turned, startled. "Mr Angove! You're just in time."

Bang!

Before Arju could say anything else, Tewksbury drew his own pistol and fired. Hitting him in the right shoulder. The big man spun and collapsed in a heap. "Tewksbury! What the hell happened?"

The Colonel ignored Eugene and started to riffle Arju's clothes. The archaeologist was bleeding profusely and groaning in pain. "Where is it?" Tewksbury was like a man possessed. "Where is it, you bastard?" He took his pistol and whipped Arju with it.

"Tewksbury, stop. For the love of God, what's wrong with you?"

"There you are... I've got it." Tewksbury stood, holding the Amulet of Shub-Niggurath like a prize.

Arju backed against a seat, clutching the exit wound just below his collar bone. Eugene and Hampton rushed over. Hampton bunched his hankie and pressed it to the wound.

"Why?" Eugene demanded. "Who do you work for."

"To keep it out of enemy hands..." Arju produced a flat stone from his pocket. It was emblazoned with a star design. It was a river stone from the Thames. The seal of the Brotherhood of Tamesis.

"What? Explain yourself?"

Click

The unmistakable sound of a revolver's hammer being cocked stopped Eugene's interrogation. He rose slowly, turning to face Colonel Tewksbury. "Stay where you are. Don't move a blasted muscle." Tewksbury grinned as he stuffed the amulet into his pocket.

"What's the meaning of this, Colonel?" Eugene asked. His voice was low and accusing.

"Power! That's what. This amulet will give the British Army the power to wipe its enemies off the map! When I call Shub-Niggurath and bring her Thousand Young to our reality, nobody will stand in our way... The Empire will rise again!"

"You're as mad as a blasted March hare!" Eugene spat. "You're no better than that SS bounder!"

"How dare you!" Tewksbury levelled the gun at Eugene's head. "I'm doing this for King and country!"

"And what if the King doesn't want a bunch of eldritch monstrosities trotting about the place, hmm?"

Tewksbury chuckled. "Oh, he will... when he sees the power of Shub-Niggurath, he will welcome me into the fold with open arms. Hell, he might even let me marry that pretty daughter of his, Elizabeth!"

"Ha!" Eugene guffawed. "I've never heard such balderdash in all my life!"

"Careful, Sir," Hampton whispered. "This man's not the full shilling."

"You really think that the King wants the minions of Shub-Niggurath at Buckingham Palace. I don't know what the Thousand Young are, but I'd wager they will make a right mess of the soft furnishings."

"Silence, oaf!" Tewksbury again pointed the gun at Eugene's head before relaxing a little. "I'm going into the next carriage, and I'm bolting this door behind me. If you try to follow me, I won't hesitate to blow your pickled brains all over the nearest seat." Tewksbury grinned maniacally as he backed away.

Eugene's taunting had not merely been for his own amusement. It was also a careful ruse to stop Tewksbury from looking behind him. Eugene's laughter had covered the sound of the door opening. The bluff chap was perfectly unaware that Sister Olive had crept up behind him with her knitting needles clasped in her right hand...

"Yow!" Tewksbury screamed as Sister Olive rammed her needles into his right buttock. He jerked forwards, losing his footing, and dropping the gun as he grabbed his posterior with both hands. As he turned unsteadily, the violent nun swung with all her weight and walloped him in the left temple with a hardback edition of the Catholic Bible.

Colonel Tewksbury hit the floor with a dull *thud.* Seconds later, Professor Mirabelle entered the carriage. "What in God's name is going on here?"

Eugene smiled as he pocketed the Colonel's revolver. "Just a bit of divine intervention, Professor... that's all."

▼▼▼

"Here, a nice cup of tea, Sir." Hampton placed the cup down on the table in front of Arju. "Do you want one, sir?"

"No, Hampton. I need something a little stronger." Eugene unscrewed the cap on his bottle of single malt and glugged a hefty measure into a teacup. "So, Arju. Are you going to enlighten us as to what the hell happened?"

"Indeed... I have been in the employ of the Brotherhood for several years now. I was ordered to accompany and protect Professor Mirabelle and the amulet at any cost. Mr Stephenson told not to trust anyone."

"Funny... that's what Edith said to me. Bloody Stephenson. This would have been a hell of a lot easier had we known we were on the same team." Eugene shook his head.

Arju nodded in agreement. "Anyway, when we met Doctor Blackburn, I instantly knew he was an imposter. You see, the real Professor Blackburn made a speech at Oxford last year. I didn't want to blow my cover, so I decided to keep an eye on him.

"Just before I joined you for supper, I heard his door open. He didn't pass mine, so I knew he was up to something. To cut a long story short, I followed him, and when I saw him take the amulet, I clobbered him with a length of lead piping. I'm afraid that I hit him a little too hard. I only meant to incapacitate him."

"But why did you take the amulet?" Hampton asked as he sat down next to Eugene.

"I didn't know who else was in on it. I thought for certain that Miss Radcliff was... poor woman. I assume that Tewksbury thought the same?"

"Indeed." Eugene nodded. "He has told me everything. The damn fellow won't shut up... He's locked up in the guard's cage, by the way... Well, when Schwarz was found dead, he hid in an empty compartment until you had gone then lurked outside while Mirabelle looked for the amulet. When he heard that it was gone, he searched the rooms. That's when he had a set-to with you, Arju. Later, when we were talking to you and Mirabelle, he snuck out after Ruby, believing her to have the amulet..."

"That's why he killed her?" Hampton asked.

"Yes. Tewksbury didn't want Ruby making a fuss while he riffled her effects. Unfortunately for him, LeBlanc saw him come out of the compartment while he was throwing up. Tewksbury knew that when Ruby was found, his valet would put two and two together... He had to be silenced. I can only imagine he took Mirabelle's dagger and Arju's braided silk to throw us off the scent... sneaky blighter."

"So, what happens now?" Arju asked.

"Well, we will be arriving in London shortly where I will hand over the amulet and Tewksbury to Edith Stephenson and her pet constables... then go and get blind drunk."

Arju laughed. "Sounds like you have it all planned

out... I should go and see Mr Stephenson."

"If you do..." Eugene smiled. "Give him a kick in the plums from me..."

Tim Mendees

Tim Mendees is a rather odd chap. He's a horror writer from Macclesfield in the North-West of England that specialises in cosmic horror and weird fiction. A lifelong fan of classic weird tales, Tim set out to bring the pulp horror of yesteryear into the 21st Century and give it a distinctly British flavour. His work has been described as the lovechild of H.P. Lovecraft and P.G. Wodehouse and is often peppered with a wry sense of humour that acts as a counterpoint to the unnerving, and often disturbing, narratives.

Tim has had over eighty published short stories and novelettes along with six stand-alone novellas and a short story collection.

When he is not arguing with the spellchecker, Tim is a goth DJ and a co-host of the Innsmouth Book Club podcast. He currently lives in Brighton & Hove with his pet crab, Gerald, and an army of stuffed octopods.

https://timmendeeswriter.wordpress.com/

https://tinyurl.com/timmendeesyoutube

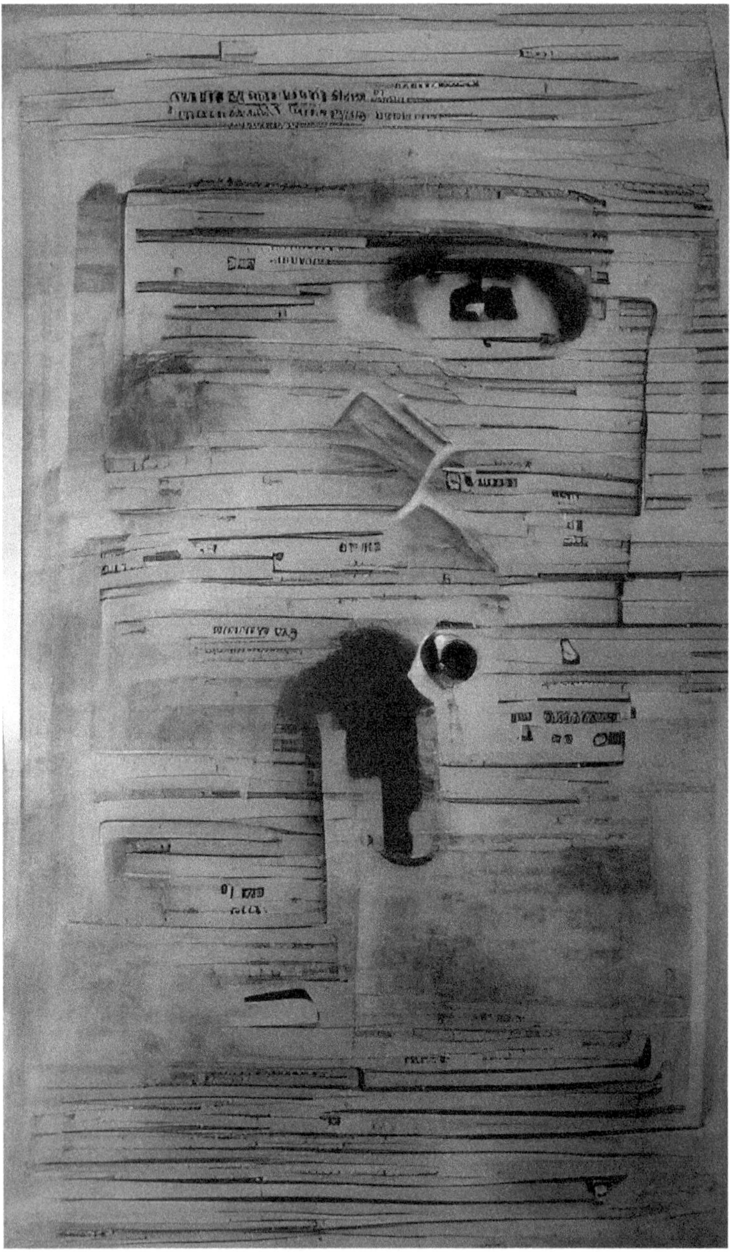

The Missing Case of the Missing Case

Charles Sartorius

It was a hot August Tuesday in my generic mid-sized city. Sweltering to be more accurate, a typical summer's day in America's heartland. I took the afternoon off from my crumby job at a mega warehouse and hopped on the public transit headed downtown. I wanted a half-day on Friday, but the boss shit canned that request; said I'd taken too many Fridays and Mondays off. I'd squandered all my vacation and sick days for the year, so I wasn't getting paid for my time away. What did the boss care? Apparently, she did. I guess Staci Holland actually gave a crap about the company, probably the only one.

I'd been taking the bus to and from the warehouse the past month in the opposite direction ever since my early seventies Vega broke down, a common occurrence. What did I expect from an aluminum block engine with over 300,000 miles and three rebuilds? I only kept the rust bucket for sentimental reasons, a hand-me-down from my late grandfather, Roscoe Nunez. He'd gotten it new as a college graduation gift back in the day and it'd been in the family ever since. A real heirloom. On my scrimpy income, I had little desire to shell out for a replacement ride. I'd planned to repair the compact Chevy in September after I'd put aside a few extra bucks. I just needed parts. I'd do the work myself, as I had little choice. Money was tight and rents high in the suburbs, even with a roommate. I could've gotten something cheaper closer to downtown, but even I had some standards. Not many.

After about an hour bus ride, I reached my destination. The office I sought was located on the first block (ground level) separating the shadier downtown area from the only slightly better, but still relatively inexpensive area of the city center — a money saver.

As I opened the door to Brass Ball Investigative Services, a blast of cold air slapped me upside the head. BBIS had popped up first on a web search for discount private investigators. Its site boasted premium service at affordable prices, coming closest to what I was actually looking for - mediocrity on the cheap.

The firm's empty lobby was sparsely furnished (a good frugal sign) with a couple of furniture warehouse knock-off couches and the most basic reception desk I'd ever encountered. The carpet appeared newer, but still threadbare, not from any wear and tear, just chintzy. This was looking more and more like my kind of establishment. A short hallway opened up directly behind the reception area, leading to a couple of offices in the rear. As I approached reception, I queried indirectly with a tentative clearing of my throat. Nothing. "Excuse me, there's a customer out front," I bellowed. You could have heard crickets chirping. "Excuse me!"

After a moment, a woman's voice responded, "I'll be out shortly." I knew from the website that BBIS ownership consisted of the Ball sisters, Crystal and Juwona; the voice probably belonged to one of them. Combined, the two siblings boasted over 20 years of related experience, taking over from their retiring dad, Harold Ball, a couple of years ago. So the experience was there. Now it was time to confirm the affordability. I was about ready to vociferate again when one of the Balls (I assumed) came clumping up the hallway as if she'd lost a high heal, a Mona Lisa smile pasted on her face. I surmised she was in the latter part of her thirties, straddling the middle-aged border. About a decade and a half my senior, with shoulder length raven hair and dark piercing eyes to match; the angular profile was not unattractive. Her contrasting tan business suit was well tailored to her slender frame, maybe a bit too expensively sophisticated for what I was looking for.

She shook my hand with a firm and confident grip. "Excuse the slight limp. I sprained it chasing down some leads in another case," she chuckled. I'm Juwona. Do you have an appointment?"

"No, and it doesn't seem necessary. Nothing was said about making one on your website."

“But it does provide a phone number; most people call first.” She appeared to be slightly perturbed by my attitude, but an empty office means never disrespecting a potential client.

“I would have, but my phone’s getting low on this month’s minutes. Can we speak somewhere in private?” Hell, anywhere in this place would be private.

With a flick of her wrist, she motioned for me to follow her down the hallway. It was a brief ramble, past the first room to the end of the hall. Her office was on the left, opposite the restroom. She ushered me into a claustrophobic workspace, brightly lit and cluttered. She was either swamped with cases or just messy and disorganized by nature. The walls were bare except for a degree in criminology from the local state university. It hung somewhat askew, directly behind her desk, adjacent to a few framed photos of Juwona posing with the ugliest French Bulldog I’d ever seen. The PI plunked down in her chair; I seated myself across from her. While moving a stack of files to get a better look at me, she handed over a business card snatched from the holder. I glanced at it, probably printed from some discount software application:

Brass Ball Investigative Services

Juwona Ball

Co-Proprietor & Private Investigator

The card also contained the standard readout like

the firm's address and contact information, as well as Juwona's license data, but no company logo, confirming I *was* in the right place.

"I can give you a few minutes if your case is a simple one. Mister?" She was scrutinizing me like a hungry wolf eyes a rabbit, a three-legged one.

"Nunez, Uriah Nunez."

"Interesting first name."

"Yours as well; my mom likes Dickens, especially his shady characters."

"Dickens?"

"Charles Dickens, the writer. I was named after Uriah Heep. Doesn't matter; just call me U like the letter. That's what I usually go by. Not to be confused with a female sheep."

"What?" She seemed a bit perplexed. Great, just what I needed, a PI who's clueless. Another potential bargaining advantage, however.

"Let's move on." I settled down into the seat as best I could. "First, I'd like to know what your fees are up front. I've done extensive research on the net and sixty dollars per hour plus expenses appear to be the going rate for this area," I lied.

"When did you look that up? Years ago?" she quipped. "We charge a very reasonable eighty-five per hour, excluding expenses, an exceptionally moderate rate. Our competition can't touch it."

"How about seventy-five dollars per hour if you solve my case and sixty-five dollars if you don't?" I countered.

"This is non-negotiable, Mr. Nunez. If you think

you can do better, there are several other PI firms in this city. You'll find them more expensive, and frankly, not as skilled as we are. My sister and I have been doing this for a long time; we can provide testimonials."

"Only from selected clientele, I bet."

"What are you implying, Mr. Nunez?"

"Please call me U. I'm implying nothing; zilch. Let me think about it for a minute. This initial consultation is free, right?"

"It was, but now I'm not so sure."

"Okay, okay; you win, but I get to review all potential expenses up front." My negotiation skills patently sucked, and I'd prematurely misjudged this lady; she was sharp. Damn.

"Of course; now what's this all about?" Juwona probed.

I was afraid I might have agreed too hastily. The eighty-five dollar per hour plus expenses was actually on the low side, according to my Internet research. I was getting a good deal.

"We're still in the consultation phase, correct?" I confirmed, trying to sound more mature and sophisticated than my twenty-five years.

"Duh; I'm not on the clock yet; how can I help you, Mr. Nunez?" she replied, more than a bit condescendingly.

"It's U."

"Me?"

"No, call me U—without the turn." I was on the fringe of exasperation with this lady.

"Let's keep this formal, Mr. Nunez; it'll be less confusing."

"Okay, Ms. Ball, as long as you won't charge me extra for the formality."

"No, but an annoyance fee is not out of the question."

I eyeballed her without a blink.

"That was ha ha," she said with a grin. "Now let's have it."

I wished to keep this as succinct and simple as possible. The easier I made it, the quicker it could be solved, I hoped. Juwona would be on the clock soon, and I wanted to make sure it didn't tick too long. I'd inherited, along with the Vega, a little over thirty grand from my dear departed grandfather. I was his only grandchild, his favorite one by default, and sole heir to the meager Nunez fortune. (Gramps skipped a generation; his will bequeathed my dad a big fat goose egg.) I could afford a PI, at least for a little while, but I hoped to keep the bulk of that dinero in a bank for down the road. Unlike my parents, I was disciplined when it came to money. I was cheap and proud of it. How cheap? If I didn't have to waste money on food to live, I wouldn't.

That's how cheap. You get no return on that particular investment except recurrent trips to the can.

"Where should I begin?" I pondered out loud.

"Well, certainly not at the end," Juwona zinged, a tinge of impatience in her voice. "How about you provide a synopsis of your situation and I'll interject with questions as needed; just the essentials, please."

We were on the same page. "It all started a couple

of years ago when my paternal grandfather, Roscoe, Sr., passed. My father, like me, was an only child. Dear old Pop always assumed he'd be the sole beneficiary of the Nunez estate but was shocked when Gramps left its entirety to me. This unexpected windfall caused me to feel badly about sometimes calling the grumpy old geezer *Grumpa* all those years behind his back, but not *that* badly. After funeral expenses and such it netted yours truly several thousand smackers plus a car." (I didn't reveal the actual sum. Juwona might get greedy.) "Gramps lived frugally, renting month-to-month a small furnished apartment in a retirement community. He seemingly possessed just a few belongings at his residence where he'd been domiciled for years. A small TV, dinnerware, clothing, and some knickknacks. He had neither cell phone nor PC. Eventually, most of his stuff I either trashed or gifted to a local charity. They were not even worth the effort of an estate sale."

"Are you sure these are pertinent essentials, Mr. Nunez?" Juwona was getting a little antsy already.

"Yup."

"Then continue but speak a little faster."

"Like an auctioneer, that fast?" This lady was a pistol. I liked her; she reminded me of me.

"No; just faster, but still comprehensible."

I proceeded, *not* accelerating my verbiage. "Well, the only items I did retain from his apartment were a couple of family photo albums, a framed autographed Farve Green Bay Packer's jersey, and Roscoe's wallet. I gave my parents the photos, but kept Grandfather's billfold, chucking it in my dresser after a cursory glance of its contents. The old cowhide contained a couple of ten-dollar bills that I pocketed and a few other things I ignored. I also kept the signed Favre jersey. I figured it would increase in value over time, especially someday when he croaked," I shared.

"I'd completely forgotten about the wallet until last week when I was cleaning out my dresser, which I do periodically. Anyway, when I came across Gramp's billfold, I decided to examine it more closely; then maybe forward the smelly old rawhide thing to my father completely empty - he'd appreciate the irony."

"Can we get to the point? I have other clients to attend to."

"Like all the ones lined up in your lobby? Business must be booming."

"Very funny, Mr. Nunez. At the moment, I've got several cases I'm working on."

"So I'm going to have to wait until you get to mine?" Juwona hadn't pocketed my money yet; I figured I could still give the PI a little grief.

"No, I'm very adept at handling concurrent cases, Mr. Nunez. I've been doing it for years; please continue." Her right shoe started tapping briskly under the desk.

"As I was saying, I began looking through it, very carefully this time. The billfold was empty except for a couple of gas and bank receipts, a Medicare insurance card, three family photos, including one of my late grandmother and him on their wedding day, and a few business cards. Gramps apparently was a cash and carry guy. No credit or debit cards for him. I checked every nook and cranny twice before placing it back empty in my dresser. I then put the family photos in my own wallet, trashing the other stuff except the business cards that would be headed for the same fate shortly."

"I assume the case revolves around one or more of the business cards, Mr. Nunez. Let's get to the gist."

"Nothing gets past you, does it, Ms. Ball? Maybe I'm not as succinct as you'd like. My bad, but we're almost there." Juwona's expression was intense enough to kindle a campfire under my behind, so I continued my narrative, this time picking up the pace a bit. "Rifling through the first three cards, I discovered two were taxi company contacts, and a third was that of an insurance broker who I phoned on the spot. She had no record of any dealings with my grandfather; couldn't even recall a Roscoe Nunez. When I got to the last business card, I noticed something I'd previously missed. It was clipped to a piece of paper meticulously folded to sit perfectly behind. While separating the business card from the clipped paper, I perused its print. It was the calling card of Sterling Nimrod, head honcho of a PI firm out of Chicago. The Sterling Nimrod & Associates business card was high end - printed in gold raised lettering along with an elaborate abstract rendition of some sort of dragon, its logo, above Mr. Nimrod's name."

"I trust you brought it with you, Mr. Nunez."

I snapped my fingers. "Crap; I knew I'd forgotten something." The expression on Juwona's face was priceless; it reminded me of a mutt painfully discovering an attempted bite of porcupine meant unanticipated consequences. "I'm messing with you. I've got it in my pack, along with that attached piece of paper."

"Mr. Nunez, you're trying my patience and wasting my day. It's time you sprinted to the finish line of this little narrative of yours."

"Okay; I unfolded the half-letter sized paper and…" At that moment, my cell buzzed. I shrugged, extending my palm out toward Juwona as I dug the phone out of my front pocket. Staci was on the line. "Sorry, Ms. Ball, I need to take this call; it's my boss."

"Make it quick, Mr. Nunez. I'll head down to the lobby and get a cup of java. Want some? It's a special blend I get from my dad."

I shook my head in the negative, taking the call from Staci. "What's up?"

"We've had several swing shift employees call in sick today; I need you to work this evening."

"But I'm on vacation this afternoon taking care of some personal business downtown."

"An unpaid vacation that ends when your shift does, as far as I'm concerned," she huffed. "I need you to get back here pronto by the beginning of the next shift; this is not an option, we're swamped. Since you've probably never cracked open the employee handbook, it stipulates I can assign you to any shift at my discretion as necessary; I can also mandate overtime as well. You may also have to work part of the graveyard shift tonight."

"Gotcha, but I'll have to catch the next transit bus out of the city center, and who knows when that'll be?"

"There's always Uber, U. I'll expect you here." With that, Staci disconnected.

I began to frantically search the transit website on

my cell for the bus schedule, as I wasn't about to waste money on a driver when Juwona walked back into the office, a steaming cup of coffee in hand.

"My boss says I have to work this evening, Ms. Ball, so I need to try and catch a bus right away. We'll have to finish this conversation later; maybe I can call you?"

"Where are you headed, Mr. Nunez? If it's north, I'm driving out that way to do some investigative work for a client."

"North is where I'm going; I work at a mega warehouse and distribution center; the one that opened a few years ago on Center Drive."

"You're in luck, Mr. Nunez; that's on my way. We can finish our conversation in the car if you'll stick to the essentials. No tangents this time. I won't even charge you for gas."

"I didn't think there were any free rides left in this world."

"There aren't; I'll take your case based on what I've heard. And yes, the car ride discussion is still part of the consultation."

Juwona was already beginning to know me too well. "I'll pull out the pertinent stuff so you can make copies. Should take you less than a minute," I said, grabbing my pack.

The PI lingered at her desk. "By the way, before we leave, I'll need a retainer of a thousand dollars upfront and completion of our standard agreement that we'll both sign. Cash or a credit card will suffice."

Geez - I knew this was coming. "I'm no whiz at math, but ten hours equates to eight hundred and fifty bucks. You think it'll take that long? It's a pretty simple case."

"There's no such thing as a simple case, Mr. Nunez, and I'm not sure exactly what the case entails yet. Things aren't always what they appear to be. I'll try my best to finish expeditiously; sometimes investigations only require a few hours. Sometimes they don't."

"Probably more don't than do," I said suspiciously. "I can have you stop at any time, right?"

"Yes, you'd owe for hours and expenses to that point. I can't promise anything, but if you're correct about its simplicity, this case could be resolved sooner than later."

"Your sooner might be my later."

"I have many former clients who will attest to my expediency, Mr. Nunez; as mentioned, I'll provide you with some references if you'd like."

"I'd only want to contact the ones you pissed off."

"There're none of those, I can assure you," Juwona retorted, her face reddening.

"Forget about it. Where do I sign?" After flashing the stink eye, Juwona handed me the paperwork, and I forked over the credit card.

With our little transaction completed, Juwona provided me a copy of the signed agreement. She then took the business card with the attached half-page I gave her and made a beeline for the copier. I stood, scooped up my pack, and ambled toward the front. She moved fast. Time obviously meant something different to her, as she was back in a flash, beating me to the lobby.

"My car's parked around the corner in the building's

garage; I'll get it and swing around to the front," Juwona said, handing me back the business card and attachment. With that, we both exited the lobby, Juwona turning to lock the front entrance.

A couple minutes passed when a late model black Lexus came screeching around the corner, pulling up next to me. I could tell immediately the return trip to work was going to be a lot faster than my scenic jaunt down here via public transit. "Nice ride," I remarked, pulling open the passenger door. After swiping a couple of doggie toys onto the floor, I plunked myself down next to my newly hired PI. "Isn't this make stolen a lot around these parts?"

"I've never had any issues; this area isn't *that* bad, Mr. Nunez," she responded, flooring the accelerator. I buckled up just as the G force jolted me back like an opposing lineman's push in an NFL playoff game.

"Okay, Mr. Nunez, let's dispense with the small talk. Continue with your so-called synopsis. I believe you left off where you were about to read the attached note. Brevity would be appreciated."

"Brief is what I'm all about; I don't like boxers." Juwona's frown told me I'd better continue the tale. "As I was saying, I unfolded the paper, perusing its contents." I paused.

"On with it!" she clamored. "I photocopied the note, but didn't really look at it because, unlike you, I'm in a hurry sometimes."

I had her riled up now. "The paper was an invoice from Nimrod for services rendered in the amount of a little over sixteen grand. It didn't contain line-by-line specifics stipulating work performed like the one I expect from you, just a brief summary of said services rendered."

"And those services were?"

It had been a while since I had a woman's undivided attention; I wanted to savor the experience. "Part of it was smudged, but what I could decipher indicated that Nimrod's firm was hired by my grandfather to locate a missing metal case stolen from his home in a burglary.

"When was the date of this invoice?"

"Over five years ago. It also stated in the summary something about surveillance on my dad, Roscoe, Jr., but that's where it became unreadable."

"It would appear from what you're telling me, your grandfather suspected his son of complicity in the burglary; either that or Nimrod was working on two distinct unrelated cases for him."

"But why would Gramps hire a PI out of state in Chicago when he lived here most of his entire life? I don't recall him ever traveling to the windy city or even talking about Chicagoland except when he was cursing the Bears."

"Bears?"

"Yes, the NFL Chicago Bears; he was a die-hard Packers fan."

"I'll surmise you attempted to contact the Nimrod agency, yes?"

"Exactly. If I could solve this enigma without the expense of a PI, I was going to do it. Motivated frugality hard at work."

"You couldn't, obviously. What happened?"

"When I got the Nimrod number from their website, I attempted to contact Sterling. I never made it past the receptionist the first five attempts, leaving a more detailed message each time. Finally, I got through to Nimrod's daughter, Nina. She'd received all my messages and actually (according to her) checked the agency's closed and inactive case files with no success. Nina also discussed my query with someone in accounts receivable. Came up with a big nada… or so she claimed."

"Did she speak with her father?"

"No, and it pissed me off. She stated her dad was a busy man and had no time for this nonsense. Nina added Mr. Nimrod wouldn't have remembered a case from five years ago anyway, as he had hundreds of old cases under his belt. With no paperwork, there was nothing more the agency could do."

"Even with the invoice number, nothing could be located?"

"Not a damn thing."

"This *is* an interesting one, Mr. Nunez - a case about a missing case, about a missing case, if I understand it correctly."

"Bingo; I can tell you graduated number one in your class."

"I did, actually. Where were you ranked in college?"

"That's classified; it's an unlisted number."

"A three-digit one, no doubt; probably four."

I let this banter slide… partly because I was losing; mostly, I wanted to get things moving. "So, what's the first step?"

"I'll contact Nimrod tomorrow; it's getting later in

the afternoon, and I find these matters are best handled early in the morning."

"You're confident you can get through to him?" I didn't want to admit she'd be better at it than me.

"I have my ways. Plus, most agencies will typically cooperate with each other to a point, depending on circumstances. There are confidentiality considerations, of course."

"You think you can wrap this up quickly?" I could envision my bank account dwindling as we spoke.

"This is a two-tiered situation, Mr. Nunez. I'll know more tomorrow."

We sat in silence for the next few minutes, each of us lost in thought. With about five minutes to go before drop-off, I inadvertently stepped on one of the doggy toys I'd hand swept onto the floor. It squeaked loudly.

"Do you have a dog, Mr. Nunez?"

"No, they're too high maintenance: costly vets, food, grooming, and cleanup."

"You don't like animals?"

"I love all creatures as long as they belong to someone else. What's your dog's name?"

"I call him Bleu."

"He doesn't share your last name, does he?" I couldn't resist.

"He's a dog; plus he's not registered to vote, so he doesn't need one," she joked.

"Naming your dog a color is kind of bizarre, isn't it?"

"Actually, it's fairly common, but it's Bleu, the French version of the hue," she drawled in a fairly decent Parisian accent.

"Makes sense for a French Bulldog; by the way, he's a looker."

"I think so; but I know he's got a face only a mother could love."

I could have returned serve with some snide remark about only a blind mother, but Juwona would be on the clock soon and I didn't want it to be with more attitude than she already had. Besides, I noticed we'd reached my destination. "You can drop me off at the next block. My prison camp's on the right," I wisecracked.

She slowed. "Here you go, Mr. Nunez. I'll give you an update tomorrow."

"Okay; remember to let me know about any costs before actual expenditure."

"You got it," she replied, letting me off then speeding away.

"Bye," I said to the lingering exhaust fumes, surprised she hadn't burned rubber. I turned and trudged toward the warehouse; it was going to be a long evening… and stuck with my boss to boot. Excellent.

The swing and subsequent graveyard shifts were endless; I wound up working the entirety of both, completely spent, as I wearily clocked out early the following morning. Because I'd been such a trooper, Staci gave me the day off to recover. Unpaid of course. But the overtime would fatten my paycheck, such as it was; I was working to pay Juwona now, motivated by the fantasy there were untold riches in Gramps' missing metal box, making all this worthwhile. I decided to start doing something I've never done before. Volunteer for overtime. Those extra greenbacks would lessen the financial impact of a PI on my paltry inheritance stash. I waited for the bus, feeling somewhat optimistic. A strange sensation indeed.

Returning to the apartment, I woofed down a bowl of oatmeal (this stuff was dirt cheap in bulk) then plopped into bed. Several hours later, I awakened suddenly from a nightmare. It faded fast but had something to do with a six-figure invoice from Juwona. I immediately checked my phone on the nightstand. No messages from the PI. Finally, at 8:47 p.m., my phone buzzed.

"Mr. Nunez, it's Ms. Ball from the agency."

"I'm sorry, you're fading in and out; who is this?"

"Juwona Ball."

"Yes; yes, Ms. Ball, what did you find out?"

"Do we really have a bad connection, Mr. Nunez?"

"Okay, you got me. I just wanted to hear you say your name."

"Why would you want that?"

"Skip it; enlighten me."

She paused a beat, the suspense killing me. "Well, I contacted the Nimrod agency this morning; you're right, Sterling's a hard guy to get a hold of. I did have a nice little chat with Nina, however. Turns out she's in the same situation I was years ago. Helping Dad out until the day when she'll take over the firm."

"You built some rapport and all that."

"Exactly; you catch on fast for a guy with an unlisted collegiate ranking." My quips were coming back to haunt me. "Anyway, she definitely remembered speaking with you; what *did* you say to her?"

"Just my usual."

"That's what I feared; it took me several minutes to smooth her ruffled feathers."

"But you eventually got that bird to sing, right?"

"You never let up, do you? More like a chirp, but we're making headway."

"And…?"

"And… she did make a half-hearted attempt to locate your father's file, and… also spoke briefly with the A/R clerk. Nina promised to engage in a more thorough search after hours tonight. She'll personally check relevant accounting files; also, after five years closed/inactive case hard copies are transferred to an outside storage facility, so she'll look into that possibility."

"Shouldn't all this stuff be on their computer system?"

"Well, that's the thing. The system was nailed by a major virus a couple of years ago, the majority of its data unrecoverable."

"Great; bad karma always seems to shadow me. What are the odds of their system getting a virus? Of all the PI agencies in all the world, Grandfather's case had to land into this one."

"*Casablanca* fan?"

"My all-time favorite flick. That and any Spike Lee film."

"As much as I hate to admit, it looks like we have something in common. It's probably the only thing."

This time I played the adult. "Let's get back to the case; our brief film discussion is costing me more than the price of a movie ticket… with popcorn."

Juwona continued, "I have one other lead. There's a

retired PI in town by the name of Knute Poindexter who used to deal with my father back in the day. He worked in the Chicago area for many years before relocating to our lovely metropolis. I phoned my dad and got his number; I'll see if he ever dealt with Nimrod."

"Great; anything else?"

"That's it. I'll check in with you tomorrow."

"Make it after 7:00 p.m.; I'm usually home from work by then, and it's much easier to talk."

"Gotcha."

"By the way, you don't mind that I'm recording our conversation, do you?

"No, I'm doing it as well. It's mentioned in the agreement."

"Nothing personal, but I want to ensure your time spent is accurately reflected on your invoice."

"That's partly why I do it. Not too many of my clients track every minute of conversation, but no problem; we're a principled agency.

"I'd track every second if it was plausible."

"Why am I not surprised? Good evening, Mr. Nunez."

I lay down on my bed, staring at the ceiling. There was much to digest, but I had to work in the morning and was still dead tired from yesterday's adventure. My digestion could wait… or should I say indigestion if I lingered too long on the monetary aspect.

The next day dragged on; I did get a bit of a respite due to Staci's absence. Apparently, she had some child care issues that couldn't be resolved, so I was forced to toil the whole day without the pleasure of seeing her smiling face. The little pleasures in life are certainly worth relishing.

Even with an hour of volunteer overtime, I made it home before 7:00 p.m. At 7:21 p.m. my phone started buzzing.

"Hello, Mr. Nunez; I trust we have a good connection like last time."

"Indeed we do, Ms. Ball; loud and clear."

"I have a business engagement shortly and we've got a lot to cover, so try not to interrupt too much and we should be able to get through it."

"Talk to me."

"First thing this morning I spoke with Nina. She conducted an exhaustive search last night and couldn't find any record of your grandfather's case file, even at their off-site storage facility. She did, however, recover that one invoice you copied for me; it was located in some stored accounting files, but that was it. The good news is said copy was completely legible, so we have a little more info regarding your grandfather's surveillance of your dad. Because your grandfather is deceased and I'd already given the impression your copy of the invoice was missing just a few lines, I convinced her to relax confidentiality parameters a smidge. After we're done tonight, I'll forward the clean invoice sent me as an attachment for your records. You're still on the call, Mr. Nunez?"

"And quiet as a tortoise."

"This is like a vacation for me. Anyway, it turns out the missing metal box and Roscoe Jr.'s surveillance cases were two separate investigations – a possibility I'd mentioned to you already. From what I can discern, Roscoe, Sr. was checking on Roscoe Jr.'s possible infidelity. The bulk of the invoice amount was linked to that investigation. Maybe your mom asked for her father-in-law's assistance, it's hard to say. Do you recall anything?"

"Five years ago I was away at college; I haven't a clue. I always assumed they had a good relationship. Sure, there were some rough patches, but overall, it was a happy household, at least when I lived at home."

"Without additional information, we won't know the details unless you query your mother…or your father."

"I think I'll let that one remain a mystery. Old ghosts might bring up new issues. I rarely see my dad anymore after Gramps passed. Mom and I meet for brunch about once a month – that's about it except for the occasional phone call. I've never been much of a family guy. Besides, I'm a bit of a disappointment to them."

"You're still young; don't give up on yourself."

"I won't; but if my dad only owned a PI agency like yours did, I'd be doing okay by now."

"You don't really mean that."

"You're right, sorry."

"I think your wit's used as camouflage. It could be better utilized channeled in a more positive direction."

"What are you, a shrink now?"

"Just saying."

"And I'm just saying please continue with today's discoveries, Ms. Ball; did Poindexter respond back to you?"

"Yes; I was just about to get to that. Poindexter called back a few hours ago and we spoke briefly. He's a little hard of hearing, but the gist of our conversation was that he's familiar with Sterling Nimrod. I'd like to go out to his home and visit with him tomorrow morning; it's only about quarter hour's drive from my office. I think I could extract a lot more information face-to-face, as it was difficult with his hearing issue to converse over the phone; he could be a key component.

"Let's see, the half hour round trip alone will cost me $42.50." The money train was pulling out of the station.

"Plus expenses, she added."

"Such as?"

"Fuel and I might need to stop for a bite."

"What's the mileage going to set me back?"

"The standard fifty-six cents per mile; it really won't amount to much."

"Okay; and since it's difficult for me to talk at work, I'll authorize an additional two hundred bucks for incidental expenses so as not to anchor the investigation." *Did I just say that?* Maybe Juwona was getting through to me…just a little.

"Great, I really don't think I'll need most of it, but sometimes the unexpected occurs. I'll keep a detailed mileage log and retain any receipts for your perusal." I could almost hear Juwona's sigh of relief.

"I'll be waiting to hear from you tomorrow evening, bye." This time I ended the call before she could get in the final word; I just had to get even.

The next workday passed as usual, excruciatingly slow and monotonously boring. I received an unexpected text from Juwona on my lunch hour while dozing in the break room, my favorite hangout in this facility: *Mr. Nunez, I'll be unable to discuss my morning meeting with Poindexter this evening as an emergency situation has just come up in another case. I'll be out of town until Sunday. Will contact u then. JB.*

A miserable day just got worse; I wasn't good at waiting. On the plus side, she'd be spending some other client's hard-earned money.

I'd volunteered for Saturday overtime, as the warehouse was still shorthanded due to a rash of absenteeism; so at least for part of the weekend I had boredom to keep me occupied. Finally, Sunday arrived and at 2:37 p.m. my phone buzzed.

"Hello, Mr. Nunez; I'm back. Ready to discuss the case?"

"I've been more than ready since Friday. Verbalize."

"Sorry about the delay, but I *do* have other cases."

"All more important than mine." I was such a pessimist.

"Not so; anyway, I think I've gotten to the bottom of things. Knute Poindexter *does* know Nimrod from his Chicago days; very well, actually. When I discussed the matter with him, he agreed to contact Sterling himself regarding your grandfather's missing files. Poindexter phoned Nimrod on his direct line. After a bit of prodding, Sterling recalled the case, but wouldn't divulge any additional details except it was one of their few out-of-state investigations at the time; a healthy portion of the sixteen grand invoice was attributed to travel and accommodations costs. He was mum on the metal case investigation, but that's to be expected."

"Crap. I thought you said you'd gotten to the bottom of things."

"I did. Although Nimrod wouldn't divulge any details about the case, he did disclose how your grandfather came upon his agency – it was through a mutual friend, one of your grandfather's old army buddies, Elrod McGillicuddy. And old McGillicuddy is alive and well, living in Florida. As soon as the Nimrod call ended, I located McGillicuddy's number and phoned him; it was an informative conversation – he tied up a bunch of loose ends as he'd been in contact with your grandfather over the years, up until his passing."

"You rock, Ms. Ball."

"Is that a compliment? It must be freezing over."

"So let's have it."

"The gist of it is Nimrod's PI never recovered Roscoe's stolen property after the police failed to do so, even after an exhaustive investigation. Your grandfather was devastated."

"Must have been a large stash of cash or other valuables," I lamented.

"No, it was filled with love letters your grandfather had gotten from your grandmother when they were dating; apparently over quite a long courtship due to his stint in Viet Nam."

"But why did Gramps hire a Chicago PI for a local job?"

"Remember, this was a dual investigation; since your dad apparently had a lot of PI friends in the area for whatever reason, your grandfather considered it prudent to bring in an outside investigator; due to McGillicuddy's input, I can provide you some details of that infidelity surveillance."

"No, that's okay. I can already guess their verdict."

"How's that?"

"Dad being aced out of the will speaks volumes."

"Understood."

"Well, there goes my dream of riches; the return on investment for this little adventure is negative. By the way, how negative?" I swallowed hard – here it comes.

"I'm happy to report you'll be getting some money back on your grand."

"Surely you jest! How much?"

"I kid you not; a few hundred, minimum. Once prepared, the itemized bill will be emailed with the exact amount."

"That eases the pain a bit; what a waste of time."

"That stolen metal case was truly priceless to your grandfather. Everything's not always dollars and cents, Mr. Nunez."

"Does that apply to your PI invoices?"

"Seriously, this experience could be much more valuable than you suspect. Maybe you'll learn a couple of life's lessons from our little endeavor; like that metal case, they can be priceless."

"Something to chew on, I suppose." *This lady actually cares about her clients...and she's freaking good!*

"Anything else?"

"Well, that about wraps it up," I concluded. "I suppose I'll be getting that little bit of moolah back shortly."

"Check's in the mail…almost. Crystal handles that side of things."

"What? She doesn't trust you with the money?" I teased.

"Of course Crystal trusts me, but she minored in accounting at the university."

"I assume she majored in fortune telling."

"You say the strangest things sometimes, Mr. Nunez."

"I guess I'm just an unconventional guy." I was going to miss this lady. "Thanks for all your help. I'll bid you adieu; if you want to add me to your client testimonials, I can embellish with the best of 'em…I'm kidding."

"Sure, but your feedback's likely sarcasm will require editing. Maybe we can discuss it over lunch sometime."

"I thought socializing with clientele would be against some kind of company policy."

"Your case is closed, Mr. Nunez…U. So technically you're no longer my client; how about we get together next Saturday at Harry's Bar & Grill adjacent to the mall; say, about noon? My dad bought the place after he retired; it was perfect for him. He didn't even need to change the establishment's moniker."

"That's right, your website mentioned his name's Harold; Harry makes sense." I bit my tongue, no more jocularity about that surname (at least not to Juwona). "Could we get a Ball family discount on lunch?" I queried hopefully.

"Of course."

"Awesome. Sounds like my kind of place. Saturday at noon it is; I'll see you then, bye."

As I disconnected, a smile stretched my lips slowly back like pulled pink taffy; an epiphany peered over the horizon. Boom! Cougars had unabashedly prowled this urban jungle for decades, but I'd never been prey before. The future just brightened considerably. And I would be having a Ball.

Charles Sartorius

Charles Sartorius has one foot in the business world and the other tiptoeing toward the literary one. An admitted project crunching workaholic with the obligatory MBA (but with an artist's soul), he does make time to write the more than occasional story and music lyric. One of his creations, *The Genome Research Project Metamorphosis*, has been accepted for publication in the upcoming 42-Word Anthology. A number of his songs appear on conventional venues such as Amazon and Apple Music. For example, the intense social commentary of *Sideswiped* and the comedic satire of *A Fart is the Best Response;* the latter judged a finalist in the 2020 USA Songwriting Competition. Originally from California, he's resided in various locales due to career opportunities including Washington, Puerto Rico, Texas, and Colorado. An avid globetrotter, he's always seeking new adventure as time and circumstances permit.

The Jog Path Killer

Vincent L. Scarsella

Sam Roth heard about it on the radio around noon as he drove home from babysitting his six year old grandson. The body of thirty-four-year-old Janice Kelso, who'd gone missing two days ago, had been found that morning in a densely wooded area of the Steinham Preserve, fifty feet off the jog path. The poor woman was found strangled to death. It was naturally suspected that, after a two-year hiatus, the Jog Path Killer had struck again.

Roth turned off the radio and grabbed his cell phone from the centre console. After fumbling around with it, he opened his contacts list and clicked the number for Detective Ray Matuszak. After four rings, Matuszak answered. "Hi, Sam. Thought you'd call. You heard."

"Yeah. So, he's back."

"Yeah, he's back. I mean, we're pretty sure it's him. I just got out here. The forensics guys are still collecting shit."

"Mind if I stop by?"

"Yeah, sure. Stop by, take a look. You still know more about this bastard than the whole task force combined."

"A lotta good it's done," Roth commented.

Matuszak didn't respond to that. Everyone knew that Sam Roth's big regret in his otherwise stellar law enforcement career before retiring a year ago was his inability to catch the Jog Path Killer.

Fifteen minutes later, Sam was standing with Matuszak in the thick woods in the midst of the Steinham Preserve at the edge of a perimeter cordoned off by yellow crime scene tape stretched around a swatch of pines and maples. Twenty yards away, the mangled body of Janice Kelso lay sprawled out on the mushy ground in a clearing amongst the brush and trees with her arms and legs stretched out this way and that. She was nude from the waist down as during the assault her sweatpants and panties had been tugged down to her ankles.

The victim had gone missing two days ago after leaving to take her regular morning jog around the 2.5-mile, narrow asphalt path that meandered through the Preserve that was only a quarter mile from her house. Her husband, John Kelso, a thirty-six-year-old lawyer in a medium-sized personal injury firm, had reported her missing shortly after arriving home at about six-thirty that same evening. He'd called the local police department after being told by one of her co-workers that she hadn't shown up for work that day as a para-legal in another law firm.

"Same MO?" Sam asked as he and Matuszak watched the forensics team swabbing the victim's body, extracting samples of whatever from the area in which it lay, and otherwise photographing the ugly scene.

"Looks it," Matuszak replied. "Probably jumped out of the woods along the path out there, grabbed her from behind, then stretched duct tape over her mouth. After that, he dragged her back here, used a nylon rope to choke her to death, then pulled down her jogging suit, panties and performed, you know…"

"...Yeah, I know."

"Anyway, yes, same MO," Matuszak said.

"Forensic guys finding anything?"

"Not sure. Hopefully, they extract enough of his saliva from her vagina for a DNA test."

"How's that going?" Sam asked. "The DNA angle?"

"Actually, I was gonna call you. It's getting promising."

"Really? How so?"

"We have a new person of interest," Matuszak said. He turned to Sam as if to let that tidbit sink in.

Sam looked at Matuszak. "Yeah? Who?"

"A Latino guy named Juan Ramos," Matuszak said. "He may've been i-deed in the Cindi Norris killing. You remember, the fourteen-year-old."

"Yeah, I remember," Sam said. She was his eighth victim, last one before Sam retired, the week before Easter two years ago. The poor kid was on her way to school, took a short-cut along the Green Ridge Park jog path.

"Well, remember the kid who happened to drive past the park on the morning the Norris girl went missing? He'd seen a white sedan speeding out of the parking lot. Couldn't recall the make of the car and didn't see the license plate. But he got a good look at the guy driving the white sedan."

"Yeah," Sam said. "Said the guy looked Italian."

Back then, that description seemed to have caused a bit of a problem. The Jog Path Killer Task Force had recovered saliva, tissue, and hair samples from three previous killings. A DNA analysis of these samples conducted by a county crime lab had indicated a 75% probability that the killer was Latino. The detectives and cops on the task force had joked for a time after that, especially in the presence of Detective Paul Andolina, that the discrepancy was no big deal as there was little difference between a "wop" and a "spic."

"His description resulted in a pretty good artist's sketch," Sam went on. "But I know all this. You said you got something new?"

"Yeah, very new," Matuszak replied. "The day after our present victim went missing, we got a call out-of-the-blue from Alan Martin, the next-door neighbour of a certain, Juan Ramos. This Martin fellow claims to have seen Ramos at around nine-thirty, three mornings ago, this past Tuesday - the same morning our current victim went missing. Martin told us that Ramos made a left turn in his late model, silver Honda CRV out of Steinham Road onto Sheridan Drive while Martin was stopped at the light on Sheridan."

"Alright."

"See, this struck Martin as funny, seeing Ramos out there that morning. Like him, Ramos lived at least a half hour drive from the intersection of Sheridan Drive and Steinham Road."

"So what was this neighbour guy doing out there?" Sam asked.

"His eighty-two-year-old mother lives in a nursing home out that way," Matuszak explained. "Claims he visits her every Tuesday morning. We checked that out and found that this Martin fellow did indeed visit his mother that morning, and every other Tuesday morning going back several weeks." He added, "Anyway, after Martin gave us this tip, I sent Andolina and Rogers out to check out Juan Ramos. They staked out his house and around noon, they followed him to a McDonald's where he ate lunch. They ordered something and sat across from him giving Andolina a chance to photograph Ramos with his cell phone. And guess who Ramos looks like."

"The Italian looking fellow in the Norris case," Sam replied.

"Bingo. A spitting image."

Sam shrugged and said, "Well, that's hardly proof enough for an arrest, let alone a conviction."

"Yeah, I know. But we've learned some other things that have perked our interest."

"Like what other things?"

"Well, like Ramos works the nightshift at the Ford Stamping Plant – eleven to seven, that's maybe only fifteen minutes from the Steinham Preserve, so he certainly had the opportunity to go hunting for prey the morning our victim here was murdered. His wife, Linda, works days – eight to four in some county job. So, during the week, they never see each other.

"On top of that, we have our ace-in-the-hole," Matuszak added.

"The DNA analysis."

"Right."

"Oh, I get it," Sam said. "What your plan is – you follow this Ramos guy around, see if you can gather some of his saliva for analysis. Secretly, of course."

"Exactly," Matuszak said. "And the neighbour, Alan Martin, told us just how we might do that. During our interview, he mentioned that the Ramos' are quiet people, mostly stay to themselves, hardly attend any of the street parties and barbecues and such. But he does know, from his few conversations with Ramos, that almost every Saturday night they go out to dinner, mostly to this Greek place, *The Stamkos Grille*, on Main Street in Orchard Grove. It's only five minutes from their house."

"Yeah, I know the place," Sam said. "Me and Karen ate there once about a year before she passed. Not bad, if you like Greek food."

"Well, tomorrow's Saturday," Matuszak said. "I'm sending Lew Krebs out there this afternoon to speak to the owner, see if he'll agree not to bus the table should the Ramos' eat there and instead let us grab Ramos' stuff – you know, his napkin, glass, fork."

Sam knew that from whatever was grabbed, they'd attempt to extract enough of Ramos' saliva for a DNA comparison from what had been found in the Norris,

Gaynor, Romanowski, and Ginelli cases. If there's a match, bingo, they'd have their man. Not only for an arrest, but a conviction. They'd finally get the Jog Path Killer off the streets.

Sam looked across at the battered corpse of Janice Kelso laying and thought that sadly, it'd be too late for her – assuming, of course, they were able to find enough of Ramos' saliva in her vagina to link his DNA to her murder as well.

"Well, at least you'd get him on four murder raps," Sam said and nodded to the corpse. "And with her, maybe five."

"We only need one match to put him away for life," said Matuszak. "And I bet you dollars-to-donuts he had something to do with all these jog path cases, including this one." Nodding to the corpse, Matuszak asked, "Wanna get a closer look?"

"Sure."

Matuszak lifted the yellow crime tape and after Sam ducked under it, they walked together toward the corpse. The forensic team was still puttering about as Matuszak approached the team leader, Paul Stevens, and asked, "Find anything?"

"Not much," Steven said. "Looks like he didn't perform, you know, after he killed her."

Matuszak glanced at Sam and said, "Well, like I said, we still have the other four."

Sam nodded emptily as he stared down at the poor woman splayed unnaturally on the ground. After a sigh, he looked down the length of her body, naked below the waist, and spotted something that gave him pause.

Frowning, he remarked, "He didn't take her panties."

Matuszak turned to him and asked, "What?"

"Her panties," Sam said, nodding to a pair of cloth panties with a flowery pattern around the victim's ankles. "He always takes them. Remember? We figured panties are his trophy for the killing, like antler's stuck on a deer hunter's wall."

Matuszak shrugged as he looked down to her ankles. Seeing the panties, he said, "Guess he didn't take them this time." He shrugged. "So?"

"So, maybe it wasn't him this time," Sam suggested with some certainty.

"It's him. His neighbour, Art Martin saw him coming from the Preserve the morning she was killed – remember? What else was Ramos doing here?"

It was Sam's turn to shrug. The two things the task force had not revealed to the press over the years was that the Jog Path Killer performed cunnilingus on the dead victim and took her panties when he left the murder scene.

"Seen enough?" Matuszak asked. "I have to get back to headquarters for a press conference just after lunch."

"Yeah, sure," Sam said. "I've seen enough."

As they started away, Matuszak asked, "You know, Sam, I was thinking about this before you got here. Would you be interested in coming back to work?"

"I'm retired, remember."

Matuszak put his arm around Sam's shoulders as they walked. "Yeah, I know," he said. "But from what I understand, you can work part-time and not have your retirement effected so long as you make under a certain threshold. And the threshold is fairly high, from what I understand?"

"For a double-dipper, yeah. Thirty-five grand," Sam said.

"You'll never make that much in the time we need to close out this case. Plus, you deserve to reap some of the glory if – no, I mean, when we make the arrest. Consider it payback for the twelve years you put in on this damned case."

"You're that confident that Ramos is the guy?"

"Call it a hunch," Matuszak said and smiled. They had reached the crime scene tape and he lifted it for Sam to duck under. "Not as good as your hunches, but pretty damn close."

As they walked to the parking lot, Sam said, "Sure, Ray, go ahead. Put in the paperwork, just for this case."

"Great, Sam. We have a briefing tomorrow morning at eight. Can you make it?"

"Yeah," Sam said. "I'll be there."

▼▼▼

At five minutes to eight the next morning, Sam Roth strolled into the briefing room and received handshakes and slaps-on-the-back from the fifteen members of the Jog Path Killer Task Force most of whom had been there when he was still in charge. Moments later, the present commander, Detective Ray Matuszak, strode in. He stood behind the podium at the front of the room and announced that Sam had been brought out of retirement, hopefully to help them carry the ball over the goal line. Everyone clapped and some made quips about his becoming a "double-dipper." After raising his hands to quiet the group, Matuszak quickly recapped the latest developments in the case and then focused on the operation planned for that Saturday evening to procure samples of Juan Ramos' saliva at *Stamkos Grille*.

After the briefing, Sam approached Matuszak at the podium and asked, "Did you find her cell phone?"

Matuszak shook his head and asked, "What? Who's cell phone?"

"The latest victim."

"Ah, no," Matuszak replied seeming taken aback a moment. "As a matter of fact, we haven't. No cell on her person, or in her car."

"Was it at home?"

"I don't know, Sam. I didn't interview Mr. Kelso. Dan and Audrey brought him the bad news, then took him out to the scene. That lasted all of two minutes. He became hysterical, bawling and what-not seeing his wife that way. That was an hour before you got there. Anyway, I don't think we've looked into that – whether she left the cell at home or where it is."

"Don't you think that's important, finding her cell? See her texts, who she may have called while she was jogging, or in the hours or days before then?"

Matuszak shrugged again. "Maybe it is and maybe it isn't. Why? Do you?"

"Well, if she wasn't killed by the Jog Path Killer, someone else had to."

"You really think that? Why, because of the panties?"

"Yeah, because of the panties," Sam replied. "Maybe it was a copycat, or even worse, someone using the Jog Path Killer's MO as cover."

"Cover? Cover for what?"

"I don't know," Sam said. "That's my point. Worst thing a good investigator can do is lock onto one and only one narrative. That's the first thing we learned in detective school."

"And maybe the Jog Path Killer took her cell phone and destroyed it figuring it was how we found the body of the Norris kid within hours of her disappearance." Matuszak laughed. "You know, Sam, I'm starting to regret bringing you back. Detective school? That was like a hundred years ago for you." He sighed and added, "But you do have a point. In fact, I'm putting you in charge of the missing cell phone. See if you can find it. Okay?"

▼▼▼

Ten minutes later, in a cubicle out in the common area of the sheriff's substation the Task Force had been using as its headquarters the last few years, Sam powered up one of their laptops. Within ten minutes, using a look-up website, he obtained Janice Kelso's cell phone number and carrier. Then, using another program, he tried locating the phone. Nothing came up.

Just before noon, while Sam was considering his next step, Matuszak came around into his cubicle and said, "Hey, some of us are running over to Charlie's for a beef on Weck. Wanna go?"

"Yeah, sure."

"How's the missing phone search going?"

"Nowhere. It's not missing, it's gone."

"Yeah, as I figured, the Jog Path Killer probably took it, then smashed it into little pieces."

"I'd still like to get the texts and numbers she called before it went missing."

"For what?"

"They may be pertinent if the Jog Path Killer isn't the one who killed her."

"Oh, Jesus, you still on that kick?" He sighed and said, "Alright, go ahead. Do what you have to do to get the texts. Now, can we go to lunch? I'm starving."

▼▼▼

After drafting a search warrant that afternoon, he drove it out to Superior Court Judge Wilkins' house to have it signed. His supporting affidavit didn't need to allege much except that the victim's cell phone had gone missing – it was not found at the scene, in her vehicle, Mr. Kelso couldn't find it after a thorough search of the house. The warrant directed the cell phone carrier to supply text messages going back as far as possible – probably five to ten days. A representative of the carrier had informed Sam that upon service of the warrant by email, they'd likely have the texts to him no later than Monday afternoon.

By late that same afternoon, Sam had emailed the warrant. He was just about to inform Matuszak when the Detective stepped into his cubicle.

"Just got some surprising and depressing news from the Janice Kelso autopsy," he told Sam. "She was pregnant."

"Oh, Jesus." Frowning, Sam asked, "And the husband didn't know?"

"Apparently not. At least, that's what he told Andolina after he delivered the news."

"How far along was she?"

"Couple months."

"How could the husband not know?"

With a shrug, Matuszak replied. "Well, he claims he didn't. She was a fairly slender woman, hid it well."

"So, what about her? She didn't know either. I don't believe that."

"Well, it is what it is. Makes it an even worse tragedy."

"Yeah, for sure," Sam agreed. After telling Matuszak about serving the text messages warrant, he asked, "We all set for tonight?"

"Yeah. I've got Peters and Jackson staking out his house. Hopefully, he and the missus will be venturing out to dinner. I mean, even if they don't go to *Stamkos,* we'll try and gather his stuff from wherever he goes."

"Sounds like a plan."

"Why don't you take off," Matuszak said. "I'll keep you posted. Don't you have a cat to take care of."

"Yeah, Ginger'll be missing me, or rather, her cat food."

▼▼▼

It went off like a charm. Juan Ramos and his wife, Linda, left their modest, three-bedroom ranch house around six-thirty and drove straight to *The Stamkos Grille.* It took them an hour and a half to eat. For five minutes after that, with some of the patrons frowning at them, Detectives Blake and Murowski collected Juan Ramos' napkin, water glass, fork, spoon, knife, and plate, and placed them into plastic baggies that were marked as evidence. They immediately drove to the office of the county crime lab where the head chemist was waiting to extract Ramos' saliva samples from the items collected at the restaurant. The head chemist promised he'd have the results of the DNA analysis by Sunday afternoon.

Matuszak called Sam around nine Saturday night and gave him the news. "Now," he said, "we can only hope and pray something comes of it."

Ginger meowed on Sam's lap as he stroked her head and said, "Yeah, hope and pray." But he thought to himself that it might not prove anything when it came to who killed Janice Kelso.

Sunday afternoon their hopes and prayers were answered. Ramos' DNA matched the saliva samples collected from the bodies of Jade Norris, Gina Gaynor, Debbie Romanowski, and Nicole Ginelli. He was the Jog Path Killer.

Matuszak called Sam and said, "We got him. It's Juan Ramos. We just made the arrest." Sam let out a laugh, feeling an odd mixture of elation and disappointment. It was like waking up on Christmas morning and getting everything you wanted from Santa Claus, but then regretting that the build up to the day was now over.

"Did he talk?"

"No. Bastard lawyered up right away," Matuszak said.

"Well, with the DNA connection, you got a solid case."

"We got more than that. When we picked him up, we executed a search warrant. And guess what we found."

"Panties," Sam said. "How many?"

"Eight."

"Bingo."

"We're holding a news conference at five," Matuszak went on. "I'd like you to be there, be on stage with the rest of the team. As I said, you deserve to be part of the party, receive some of the glory for all the work you put in over twelve years."

"Sure, Ray," Sam said. "I'll come down. But we still have some work to do on the Kelso case."

"You are stubborn, you know that. Friggin' relentless."

▼▼▼

On Monday afternoon, the carrier emailed Sam the text messages recovered from Janice Kelso's cell phone for the five days preceding her murder. He printed them, placed them in a folder, then left his cubicle for Detective Matuszak's office. When Sam walked in, Matuszak was just getting off the phone.

"Hi, Sam. Come on in, sit," he said and pointed to the chair before his desk. "I just got off the phone with Ralph Schuster, you know, the ADA who's handling the

Ramos prosecution."

"Best in the office."

"That he is," agreed Matuszak. "Anyway, he just got off the phone with Nick Orsini, Ramos' lawyer. Ramos wants to confess. To everything. All nine killings, including our latest, Janice Kelso. Schuster and I and the Police Commissioner are meeting with him at Orsini's office tonight at six. Apparently, the DA and Orsini worked something out about having Ramos admit everything in exchange for spending the rest of his life in a facility close by instead off across the state. This way, it'll be easier for his family to visit him. Ramos has three brothers and a sister who live here. Not to mention his wife."

"His wife would still visit him after this?"

Matuszak shrugged. "You know what they say, love is blind."

"She didn't know a thing?"

"I talked to her myself right after we arrested him," Matuszak said. "She was stunned. I mean, the woman couldn't function. And the facts are that he killed all these poor girls every two, three, four years apart on the mornings after he left his shift at Ford and after she'd left home for work. Anyway, I don't think she had a clue about any of this." He frowned and asked, "Now, what do you got?"

"Proof, I think, that if Ramos confesses to killing Janice Kelso, it's bullshit."

"Like what proof?"

Sam opened the folder on his lap, held up the printout and said, "These. Texts Janice Kelso sent to, and received from one, Mark Tarnowski, a guy with whom Janice was apparently having an affair at the time of her murder. I did a quick search on the internet, checked this Tarnowski fellow out. He's married, two little kids, daughters. He's a lawyer who works in the same firm as Janice Kelso."

He lifted the printouts he'd brought to Matuszak's office. "For example," he

said. "From five days ago, from her to him:

I WAS RIGHT. TEST WAS +.
HAVING YR BABY. R BABY.

"And then, Mark's reply:

SHIT. THIS IS BAD BAD BAD BAD.
THIS CAN'T HAPPEN.
IT UPSETS TOO MANY LIVES.
WE HAVE TO STOP IT.

"Her response:

STOP IT? ABORT? NO NO NO NO. I WON'T!
CAN'T BELIEVE U JUST SAID THAT.

"Then, him:

IT'LL RUIN OUR LIVES. TOO MANY LIVES.

"Her:

YOU MEAN UR LIFE.
HAVING YR BABY BEST THING FOR ME.
I LOVE YOU. YOU DON'T ME?

"Him:

YES, I DO. I'M JUST, STUNNED.

"You getting this, Ray?" Sam asked. "Now, we have a guy with a motive. And opportunity. According to Mr. Kelso, she left the house for her jog at eight. He left at eight-fifteen for the office. That gave Tarnowski plenty of time to hide in the woods, surprise his pregnant mistress and kill her. Make it look like the Jog Path Killer. Except he didn't know about the panties. So he left them."

"Sam, I think you been watching too many crime shows on TV," Matuszak said with a laugh. "This guy had time to do all that, commit a heinous murder, and get to work on time."

"We don't know when he got to work that morning," Sam replied. "He's a junior partner at Lambert and Waverly. That's a big firm. He's a lawyer. He doesn't punch a clock." He sighed and added, "Anyway, suffer an old cop's fancy and ask the medical examiner to take a blood sample from that poor foetus so we can do another DNA analysis. See who's baby it was."

After another sigh, Sam said, "And, anyway, I have another reason asking for that."

"What other reason?"

"I think Mr. Kelso should also be considered a person-of-interest."

"Oh, Jesus, Sam."

"No, listen." Sam shook the printouts and said, "A short time after her exchange of texts with Tarnowski, Janice Kelso texted Mr. Kelso, asking for a divorce." Sam looked down and read from the paper in his hand, "'It's over, Jack. I have no love for you in my heart – if I ever truly did. I love someone else and I'm pregnant with his baby. His baby! A baby you couldn't give me. And so, it's over. All I ask is for my fair share after thirteen years of marriage. I know what I'm entitled to. And remember, I have a lot to tell people about your weird sexual interests, so don't think you can play hardball. Goodbye, Jack. Please don't call me. See you in court, as you like to say.'" Looking up, Sam said, "Pretty cold, hey?"

"Yeah, cold," Matuszak agreed. He laughed and added, "Cold as my ex-wife."

"So, we've got another guy," Sam went on, "with a motive to kill Janice Kelso – Jack Kelso. I mean, he must earn high six figures at his firm, and thirteen years of marriage was going to entitle Mrs. Kelso to a hefty divorce settlement. Not to mention whatever secrets she knew about his weird sexual interests, whatever they were."

"But aren't you forgetting something?" Matuszak asked. "Aside from the fact that Juan Ramos, the real Jog Path Killer, will be confessing to killing Janice Kelso, he was spotted by his neighbour on the morning of the killing near the very scene of the crime."

Sam frowned and replied, "Yeah, sure. I know that." He shook his head. "It's coincidence, pure dumb coincidence. Maybe he was out there scouting out the place, planning his next murder there. Only, he got beat to it by either Mark Tarnowski or Jack Kelso."

"So let me get this straight," Matuszak said. "You're saying we now have three suspects in the Janice Kelso murder – Juan Ramos, of course, as well as Tarnowski and Kelso."

"Yeah, that's exactly what I'm saying."

Matuszak shook his head. "You tell anyone else this cockamamie theory?"

"Of course not. Only you."

"Good. Keep it that way for now, okay? Let me think it over."

"Yeah, sure."

"There is one major problem with your theory even if you are right," Matuszak said.

"What's that?"

"Proving it."

▼▼▼

At eight o'clock Tuesday morning, Sam showed up for the Jog Path Killer Task Force briefing already having learned from a news conference held Monday night that Juan Ramos had confessed to the nine Jog Path Killer murders. With a wide grin, Matuszak held up the morning edition of the city newspaper with the front-page headline blaring:

JUAN RAMOS IS THE JOG PATH KILLER
CONFESSES TO NINE MURDERS

Everyone cheered and patted each other on the back. After they settled down, Matuszak announced that, in light of the arrest and likely forthcoming guilty plea, the Task Force would be dissolved. Choking up, he thanked everyone for their dedication and hard work that finally brought the Jog Path Killer to justice. Nodding to Sam, he added that it was especially gratifying to have him back on the team when, at long last, they'd caught the killer.

Immediately after the briefing, Sam strode into Matuszak's office. After sitting in the chair before his desk, he said, "I was wondering what Ramos said about the panties in the Kelso case. Why he left them."

"He didn't say anything," Matuszak said. "And to be honest, Schuster didn't push it. He described her strangling pretty much like he did the others – grabbed her from behind, stretched duct tape over her mouth, the nylon garret and all the rest. Then, the pleasure he took in strangling the life out of her. Real sick shit."

Sam shook his head and after staring down at this lap for a time, looked up and said, "So that's it?"

"What do you want? He confessed."

"I'd like to interview him."

"Who? Ramos? No, Sam, you can't."

"Why not? If I can get him to recant…"

"You're not getting him to recant," Matuszak said. "That's ridiculous. Schuster would have my head. The

DA would have my head. No, you need to leave well enough alone."

"Well enough alone? You could live with that? Knowing that maybe someone got away with murder?"

"Sam, its pure speculation on your part, based on a series of texts proving nothing more than a sordid lover's triangle. They don't prove that Mr. Kelso or that other fellow…"

"Tarnowski."

"Whatever. They don't prove that either of them murdered Janice Kelso. Ramos confessed to it. He was observed near the scene of the crime within minutes of its commission. The MO was the Jog Path Killer's MO."

"Except for the panties."

"You're a stubborn son-of-a-bitch, you know that?"

"You know, of course, that what I found is *Brady* material."

Matuszak glared at his old friend. "What?"

"You know," Sam explained, "*Brady* material. Information favourable to the defence. My findings might exculpate Ramos. We have to let Nick Orsini know." He smiled and added, "Right?

"You son-of-a-bitch." Matuszak sighed. "You know what? Write me up a goddamn report outlining what you found. Get to it me by this afternoon. I'll run it by Schuster. See what he wants to do. You alright with that?"

"Yeah, sure, Ray. Thanks."

Late that afternoon, Matuszak dropped by Sam's cubicle. He told him that after skimming Sam's report, Schuster had conferred with the DA and they had reluctantly agreed to divulge its findings to Nick Orsini; and, provided Orsini agreed, Sam and Matuszak could interview Juan Ramos.

▼▼▼

The following afternoon, Sam and Matuszak walked into the grim, consultation cell with grey cinderblock walls in the downtown holding centre run by county sheriff's department. Ramos was sitting next to Nick Orsini. After Sam revealed his doubts about his being involved in the Janice Kelso murder, Ramos looked at Orsini and moment, then turned to Sam. He smiled then said, "No, you're wrong, Detective. I killed her. I killed them all."

On the ride back to the Task Force headquarters, Matuszak said, "So, you satisfied?"

"No, Ray, I'm not satisfied," Sam said. "Even though that scumbag didn't recant, I still don't think he killed the Kelso woman. He's still playing the plea bargain game. Now, I'd like to interview Mark Tarnowski and Jack Kelso. You know, surprise them with the texts and try some old tried and true techniques to slip them up."

"Like what techniques?"

"Lie to them. Ask them to explain these texts, then ask them why they weren't at work on time that morning and tell them they were seen near the Steinham Preserve around the time of the murder. Lies like that. See how they react. An offer of an explanation, any explanation, may give us sufficient cause to go further, maybe even get a search warrant."

"A search warrant for what?" Matuszak asked.

"Their homes," Sam said. "Grab their computers. See if they've been researching the Jog Path Killer on the internet – you know, how he did his murders. I mean there's been a lot written on the case over the last twelve years. Both Tarnowski and Kelso knew Janice ran in the preserve weekday mornings before work. So it would be a perfect fit – make us think that it was the Jog Path Killer. Except Tarnowski and Kelso didn't know about the panties. That was never on the internet."

"Well, Sam," Matuszak said, "sounds like a well-thought-out investigative plan. Only, you'll have to do it on your own time. I've been directed to cut you loose, effective immediately."

With a laugh, Sam asked, "You firing me?"

"No, I'm re-retiring you," Matuszak said. "Sending you back to the world where every day is Saturday." As they turned into the Task Force headquarters parking lot, he added, "It's kind of funny, isn't it? Ironic. Here you spent the last twelve years tortured by your failure to catch the Jog Path Killer and now, after he's caught, you're tortured by another jog path killer."

With a laugh, Sam replied, "Yeah, I'm the master of ironies." As Matuszak pulled the unmarked sedan into his reserved parking space, Sam added, "But just like I had faith, or almost always did, that something would come up, and we'd catch the original Jog Path Killer, I have faith that something'll come up and we'll catch the real Jog Path Killer who killed Janice Kelso. Something unexpected. One of them, Tarnowski or Kelso, will slip up, say something to someone, admit what he did, thinking the coast is clear. I don't know, whatever. Something."

After a deep sigh, he said, "But for now, the jog path killer is still out there. Guilty as sin."

Vincent L. Scarsella

Vince Scarsella has ten novels and three short story collections to his credit in the crime/mystery and speculative fiction genres, including the Amazon bestselling Lawyers Gone Bad and The Anonymous Man series. These works are available at Amazon.com.

Numerous of his short stories have appeared in print and online magazines such as *The Mystery Tribune* and *The Leading Edge*, as well as in numerous print anthologies. He is also a regular contributor to Amazon's Kindle Vella publishing platform. His short story, "The Cards of Unknown Players," was nominated for The Pushcart Prize.

His plays, "Hate Crime," "Practical Time Travel," "Last Love," "The Penitent," "The Walrus Was Paul – A Beatles Sing-Along," and "Land of the Greedy Mouse" have been staged at colleges and community theatres. "Hate Crime" has been accepted with five other plays for the Tampa Bay Theatre Festival 2022 and will be staged in Tampa from September 2-4, 2022.

Moroccan Murder Mystery

Rekah Valliappan

What a lot of funny people it does take to make a world.

--Agatha Christie

The plan suddenly made sense. Early in December I arrived at the hill resort town of Genting Highlands to rest before my onward journey to Oswego, my home-town in America. I was expecting to fully relax after my sudden bout of pneumonia in Bangkok, which had set me back in my travels by several weeks. Coupled with a foreignness taking toll at a longer than intended stay, a strange malaise seized me. My late husband had known the place well, as he had made a number of business trips there over the years.

"You'll like it. The Thais are very friendly, you'll see," he used to say in that roguish way he reserved for me. I had liked living in Bangkok, nice enough sort of place, within help and easy reach of Malaysian friends looking to spend a few days for lively stopovers, frequent getaways to Sentosa island. Jim had mingled in high government circles with grand parties at the houses of Thai royalty. Unfortunately, the days flew by, and I found that the moon in Saturn would not allow my prolonged stay in the hills. My first week in Genting Highlands was a disaster, made exceedingly miserable by heavy torrential rains and intermittent fog so dense I scarcely left my room. Having exhausted my stock-pile of better lifestyle magazines and conversed to the hilt with all the guests in the hotel willing to listen to a cantankerous middle-aged woman with no more stories to relate, I began to miss home, my cello practice which I had taken up in my retirement, and my sound proof rooms which afforded me the luxury of a certain kind of peace and quiet I craved.

Soon I began to feel the creeping signs of discomfort coming over me. I have never been one to take my doctor's advice seriously. That's the way I was going to stay. Not even on that memorable occasion when I had wrongly surmised a complete recovery from a bad case of stomach flu so severe I could scarcely walk, let alone climb. I had proceeded on a long trek to the salt pools of Maras, highly recommended for a photography lover such as myself. I was out stone cold for a good thirty-six hours. A fairly common case of hereditary mood swings mixed with bullheadedness. Runs in certain families, my doctor concluded, none too pleased.

I was ready to leave Genting Highlands without delay, to take the first train, bus, cab or boat to somewhere sunnier, when an acquaintance of mine from the London days, back when I was a student of elementary mineralogy and he a young radical studying history, now a well-renowned collector of rare stones and rocks, came to the rescue with an invitation to his mansion in Penang. I had not seen him in decades. Never one to mince words he greeted me in typical fashion.

"Gigi!" he exclaimed, his age-old pet name for me, since he could never get the hang of Jeeveetha, "I do believe you have added a full twenty pounds since last I saw you. Very becoming."

"I had thought it more like two or three," I mumbled after a chuckle, blushing slightly. Pleased he'd noticed, and glad to see him looking so well and as jovial as ever. For he had added no weight, was well turned out, his Oriental face beaming out under the peak of his yachting cap, and his hair only slightly peppered. The first northbound train out of Kuala Lumpur saw me on it, my plan to leave materialized, my hopes restored.

My destination was appropriately called Old Hutton Hall since the restoration which gave it heritage status held within its blue painted walls the most amazing granite and metamorphic schist specimens mounted to scale and preserved in glass cases, along with a remarkable collection of ancient books in a museum sort of set-up. My sentiments softened to even keel. They seemed to hold for me the immediate promise of sunnier days. I could fancy myself in digs outside Chichen Itza to survey the stone, or on a dazzling river cruise of the sun-scorched Chao Phraya waterway. Now *this.*

The mansion of Sir Wilkie Tang resembled a grand hotel more than an old family dwelling. With thirty-odd rooms of exquisite architecture, the largest of which was called the Morocco Room as I described, was filled with all manner of strange relics, replicas of chedi in brass, sedimentary rock and mementos from Egypt, Peru, Oman, the Salisbury crags of the Scottish Highlands. Hundreds of leather-bound books loomed out of high shadowed shelves. An overstuffed chair stood by the larger of two bay windows collecting a dusty stream of sunlight filtering through the bamboo blinds. This priceless room I was shown immediately upon my arrival. Sir Wilkie took particular delight in introducing me to his impressive array of exhibits, hovering over each tool, big and small basalt and dolerite volcanic rocks laid out in orderly glass showcases. I was suitably impressed, although filled with a little unease at his vast collection of odd finds. He had not changed at all was my initial thought. His passion was undiminished. I was also quick to notice how oftentimes lonely men become exceedingly attached to their earthly possessions and surroundings to the extent they want for nothing else, not even family. I found this to be the case and the very same reason why my friend of the old days had not changed. However, with true English wit, which he retained from his London days, perhaps satisfied with the range of expressions he captured on my face, he set my unease aside, jesting with me light-heartedly that one day he may wake up in the dead of night in the midst of all this fantasy setting of rocks as a Himalayan *yeti*, or a Baskerville hellhound which he most dreaded, or even the legendary *nessie*.

So, on the evening of my arrival we were sitting for dinner on the veranda, the weather having turned cool and damp as if angry with me for trying to get away from Genting Highlands up in the hills, the bowing servants had liberally laid out a magnificent spread and retired, when Sir Wilkie threw me a strange crime puzzle.

Old Wilkie, for that was his pet name in our London days was not a bad fellow—extremely long-winded of course, like most Singaporeans--fond of telling endless long stories and playing jokes and laughing out loud at his own comedy. And he had another most peculiar habit of requiring precise and prompt answers in return, which he would proceed to systematically deconstruct. What is the square root of *pi?* How many angles has an obtuse triangle? How many vertices in a prism? Expected his friends to reply like walking encyclopaedias.

"My dear Sir Sherlock Holmes," I replied with equanimity, more to humour him for taking the pains to provide me the entertainment to make up for the dismal weather, at the same time trying to sound jocular and barely able to conceal my glee that he should relive the fun student days of our time in London "You should know this is the very talk that ensures my keenest interest."

Recognizing I meant it in jest of course, my host and I joked for a bit on crime in the 21st century, the reappearance and disappearance of some of the most famous works of art in the art world, how the body count had so much reduced in all corners of the world, thanks to efficient police work aided by clever detective work and international policing, there was not much by way of excitement any more, not even in cosy locked rooms. Murders of varying degrees had practically vanished or grown terribly unfashionable.

The words had barely left my mouth when in moments Old Wilkie grew serious. Gone was the laughter, his voice sombrely warming up to his favourite theme.

"But there *are* crimes and by Jove certainly crimes other than murder one can think of, are there not? Surely, there's fraud and theft and unsolved mysteries."

It was as if he was seeking my approval. I agreed, nodding thoughtfully, not at first catching on where this was headed

"Nothing to it, if murder is to be replaced Sir Wilkie."

"Is there no place at all for robbery?" he asked with such an inflexion to his voice

I gathered there was more to his casual question than he was letting on.

"Such as?" I laughed with a wave of my two hands at the circling mosquito after my blood. It was the twilight hour which attracted the most insects. I had a particular dread of dengue having lost Jim to the haemorrha-gic fever years ago, and we were seated in the open veranda.

Sir Wilkie stared at me intently albeit absentminde-dly, as if dismissing from his mind the inappropriateness of having to reveal what he should. Then having decided, he continued in all seriousness.

"My good luck mascot I called it the moment it arrived. My dear friend, if what you're about to reveal is a real theft, I should send for the police at once, the real police."

"Yes--yes, that too," Old Wilkie replied distractedly, as if those aspects were the least of his worries, "--worth over nine hundred thousand pounds . . ."

"Oh my," I said, sounding alarmed "What's that in *ringgit*?" I had spent far too many years in America to understand the present-day currency exchanges.

His dark eyelashes quivered. "With my expertise in ancient materials, scripts and rock collection I was the happiest man in Morocco to be the one and only Singaporean in possession of such rare, salvaged items in the lost and found market. Who wouldn't?"

"Tell me, is the crime puzzle to be an historical one too?" I queried, making sincere attempts to get to the heart of the matter, for truth to say I was lost, completely at sea as to what he was making veiled reference.

"No," Sir Wilkie replied "not as in Egyptian antiquities history if that's what you mean, or rather in a way when you think of its ancientness. It had to do with a sealed Moroccan chest in a locked Morocco Room."

To sum up Old Wilkie's narrative from the story as it unfolded, it seems one Altaf Gazra Ben-Chodo, a merchant of a hundred languages, a dozen countries, and of ill repute to boot, owned a large curiosity shop called *The Flying Carpet Antiques Gallery* in the Husni quarter, not far from the al-Bashir Mosque. He knew the art of making a killing from anyone of substantial means. Sir Wilkie acquired from this wily merchant several old stone gabbro rocks and one locked Moroccan chest which contained another rock of unimaginable value, the entire collection stored in one large room which was sealed. It is a common practice when dealing with second-hand merchants to haggle hard for their goods. Every buyer and seller knows these shoppers' rules. Items sold are marked up at ridiculous prices. On this occasion Sir Wilkie was either too excited or too inebriated. He forgot the prerequisites of a purchase formula. The allure of a locked chest was much too strong even for one as hardy in these dealings as him. He willingly paid the price demanded to be on his way, which must have been noticed by the merchant and others around him, who knew how to spot a customer not accustomed to haggling nor used to the risky selling practices of fly-by-night shops getting rid of stolen merchandize, finds ancient artifacts and all manner of rare unheard of together with general bric-a-brac, all with no price tags on them.

Such large heavy rocks could only be moved by se-curing the appropriate heavy machinery, so Sir Wilkie left the purchased goods overnight in the storage room of *The Flying Carpet*. The owner assured it was the safest room in entire Morocco and kept securely locked at all times, not even Ali Baba could access. That same night with the merchant being away on customary bu-siness, holding the only duplicate set of keys, the shop was visited by a gang of expert thieves. With complete disregard for legend, archaeology or value, the Moroc-co room was ransacked, the handcrafted Moroccan chest was pried open and plundered for its precious content, while the rest of the large rocks were left untouched.

"What was in the chest?" I demanded to know, my interest peaking sky-high, "of such immense value that even thieves would disregard the gabbro rocks of equal value?"

It seems this strange rock placed for safe keeping in the Moroccan chest was reputed to be none other than the last mined moon rock collected by the failed Voyager on their moon mission, which crash landed. "Its great value lies in its high platinum content, more valuable than a pound of gold of equal weight," said my host tonelessly.

"And the gabbro rocks?" I asked, puzzled, "What of their intrinsic content?"

"Almost the same in age and texture, over four billion years old and in colour of a similar pewter grey, but with plutonium, silver, gold traces and other minerals in the mix, except that the rock in the chest was of the moon's crust, the others not in the chest were of the earth's crust."

"And are you certain of this rare moon rock in the Moroccan chest?" Sir Wilkie cleared the matter in a few minutes. His purposeful conversation with the merchant had reassured him as to the authenticity of the rocks he was purchasing and ensured the quality of the goods. By golly he was as certain as could be.

"And this one is just as I requested, from the moon's underside?" Sir Wilkie had asked Ben-Chodo in a cordial manner, pointing specifically to the beautifully handcrafted Moroccan chest.

"Finest grade moon rock, Effendi!" the merchant had replied, with, I assumed, an oily smile and exuding graciousness. Never having visited Morocco I tried to picture the scene from some old movie re-runs flashing through my mind.

"And over the telephone you mentioned the location on the moon as being the crater--maria?"

"Dark moon, ey Effendi!" had said the merchant rubbing his hands, doubtless at the nature of the juicy deal and the lucrative shift of money about to change hands.

I professed to having small knowledge of the moon rock market much less its value, to which Old Wilkie enlightened, the subject being his favourite. The next half hour passed blissfully in an edifying lecture on lunar surfaces, its lacus, palus and sinus, features I was unaware with all the knowledge of mineralogy I possessed. The moon was more than a silver orbed maiden of poetry books Sir Wilkie informed with a little twinkle in his eye. Twenty years after 900 lbs. of moon rocks brought back to earth went missing, their value had gone up by a thousand-fold. No question if the rocks were genuine. Altaf Gazra Ben-Chodo's word was as gold in the marketplace. After the merchant had confirmed the goods, it was left to Old Wilkie to seal the deal and be on his way. Not one to purchase on impulse, satisfied with his qualitative research and a sense of good feeling, he was absolutely certain he had got himself a flattering bargain.

For days following the theft Sir Wilkie Tang was inconsolable. In shock. He raged with an unknown fever that lasted a week. Thankfully, he recovered. The moment he did he rushed to the old antiques shop to confront the merchant of the crime. He was in a real quandary breaking out with shivers and sweats. The merchant had vanished. *The Flying Carpet* was closed. Having absconded with two gains on the same transaction Old Wilkie was convinced the rogue merchant would not be found, neither would the moon rock, nor his money.

"What a let-down!" I concluded in earnest sharing his sentiments. "You think you have something of real value, and it disappears. You are cheated of it. No money and no goods. Great shame! But it's an all too familiar story I can tell you."

Sir Wilkie remained in Morocco for a whole month dealing with the local police whose support he had secured, handling errand boys sent undercover to gain word of the whereabouts of the merchant. But none was found. The tell-tale signs of foul play staged in the antiques shop turned out to be fake clues, to fool the investigators. Overturned tables, collectibles either broken or tossed here and there to indicate a fight had broken out. All were fake. The dark red smears found on the broken Moroccan chest suggesting a life and death struggle had turned out to be nothing more than vermillion powder dust mixed with grease traces to look like bloodstains.

"The scoundrel made away with the goods which rightfully belonged to me," Sir Wilkie said petulantly, for the tenth time, a faraway look in his eyes, as if the act of thieving was the harder to bear than the actual financial loss he suffered. He laid his large hand for comfort on his familiar dragon-headed *Foo* dogs protecting the entryway to his veranda. He sighed deeply multiple times.

"There are lots of unscrupulous dealers around unloading bogus paintings and stuff," I commiserated as best I could. Not being a victim myself I could sympathize.

"Morocco is a large kingdom. But small, in the way people talk," said Sir Wilkie as if trying to explain a universal phenomenon. "Stories emerged the merchant had met with a just fate, taken before the *Cadi* judge for his crimes and decapitated."

"Gossip is everywhere my friend, and so is unkindness," I replied, "Worldwide. People who have nothing better to do, gossip. Unsentimental news, but true," I could only hope my remarks would give him some solace.

"My surmise was had the merchant Ben-Chodo died an unnatural death the authorities would have heard of it. Nothing was heard. Even years after the incident nothing has come to light with the international police on watch in every country. Likely he has set up shop somewhere on this planet and is enjoying his ill-gotten gains in Tahiti, Tonga, or Timbuktu. Who knows?"

Dinner was over. The servants had cleared the tables. The night was pleasant and cool. The scent of frangipani filled the air. The rain had stopped. Reluctant to retire after the long tale we sipped a nightcap, a cognac shot for him and hand-rolled *oolong* green tea for me.

"This business of the stolen moon rock has obviously caused you a good deal of pain. You are sure the facts are exactly as you have told me?" I asked, unwilling to let the subject of our entire dinner slide into oblivion

Sir Wilkie grew silent for a while. At length he said "I don't think I've left out anything. That wretched fellow had cleaned out, lock, stock and barrel. Not even the shop remained. Not a sign of goods in *The Flying Carpet* Gallery. I'll swear to you my moon rock was nowhere in Morocco. And neither was Ben-Chodo."

Old Wilkie's face looked distressed re-living his old story which he had not visited for decades I suspect, but chose to since I an old trusted friend had chanced to stop by, as if he was an unfortunate specialist in the topic of unhappiness. I did not think it a fortuitous circumstance on my part to press for more. "Quite so," I said, waving away politely the mint chocolates offered, while he lit a cigar.

"I must admit our scientific training controls our destinies. The moon rock which I dearly craved evaporated into the hot dry air of the Husni quarter that accursed day. I salvaged what I could of the rest, my untouched gabbro rocks. I personally accompanied the cargo to Malaysia, by ship, as speedily as I could leave, willingly assisted by the helpful authorities, never to set foot in Morocco again. Here my woeful story ends, Gigi."

My host's distressful tale kept me awake long after we had parted for the night. Unable to sleep I turned and tossed in my comfortable four-poster bed. I paced the large guest room given to me. The mansion was quiet. Occasionally, the sound of cicadas broke the quiet night air. A restlessness overtook me. I took a few wrong turns down passages and landings, unfamiliar with the house and its many rooms. The household had retired for the night. Only after paying one more visit to Sir Wilkie's famous Morocco Room did I grow drowsy enough to finally rest. In moments I dropped off into a long dream-filled sleep, leaping over silvery moon mountains.

In the morning a promise of bright sunshine and blue skies made me hope for the best to complete the rest of my sunny stay in Penang. I was eager to revisit the Snake Temple where Jim and I had our pictures taken holding a couple of sluggish vipers knocked out by the heavy fumes of incense which burnt at all hours. After a brisk walk in the spacious tree-filled grounds, a chat with the gardeners on the best ways to grow laburnum and hibiscus and a particular species of orchid, I greeted Sir Wilkie at the breakfast table, famished, and having worked up an appetite. Over some excellent half-boiled eggs, dumplings and *dim sum* I informed him that I had solved the crime.

His astonishment was acute. First, he laughed heartily, concluding my remark was in jest and meant to humour him, since it was, he who had thrown the challenge the previous day. When he gathered, I meant what I said in dead earnest, he looked so excited it made me wish all the more to show off my detective cleverness.

"It all came to me," I said, equally excited, "after some spooked dreams of moon maidens, lunar craters, devil dogs and even Loch Ness monsters. I intend to explain but must first ask you trust what I do or say when we visit the Morocco Room."

We were both too excited to eat to our heart's content. Within minutes we were standing before the glass cases mounted by rich symbols representing billions of years' old crusts. To my host's gasping disbelief and without any explanation I leant over and broke the glass seals. Having broken ten seals, I attempted to chip away at each rock with the use of a garden pick I had borrowed from one of the gardeners earlier. It was fortunate for me that Sir Wilkie while thinking me brilliant was conveniently frozen on the spot, mouth hanging open, eyes bulging as if they would shoot out of their sockets, too astonished to move or cane me over the head with one of his own garden instruments.

Having temporarily completed what I had set out to do I exposed the different gabbro rocks. At first Old Wilkie showed evident scepticism and disappointment, I might add even a trace of effrontery that the shorn crusts all looked the same. I had heard the night before how unscrupulous merchants interchange the rocks in order to exact a higher price.

Watching me at work Old Wilkie's amazement at Ben-Chodo's trickery was visibly rekindled. Red-faced and incredulous my host cried out "That I should have been taken in by a counterfeiter, as well as a thief!"

"Fear not your reputation, Sir Wilkie, it happens to the best of us," I reassured him, scraping away industriously at each rock, till traces of emerald-green were visible. "This is not a cheap handiwork."

In half an hour each one of the rocks had been somewhat exposed to prove that he had been deceived. Old Wilkie's distrust and anger mounted at the perfidy of the merchant, at me for ruining his precious rocks collection, at the world in general. "Really, Gigi!" he thundered, enraged in face. "You have gone too far! You have ruined an entire collection to prove that these were ordinary slabs of dark carbon rocks and not the volcanic ones thrown up by tectonic forces?!"

"No. On the contrary I have exposed a most diabolically conceived and concealed theft of mineralized rocks, committed during your stay in Morocco."

Sir Wilkie gasped as one struck by a bolt of lightning, "What are you saying?"

For the better part of two hours, I spoke to my host, first assisting him in recovering from the shock, then explaining how I had arrived at my mad conclusions, which made little sense, even to me.

"I first suspected the truth Sir Wilkie when you mentioned the gabbro rocks and other objects you obtained from Ben-Chodo had been left untouched during the botched robbery in the locked Morocco room. My suspicions increased in light of this revelation. Did it not strike you as unusual that your ship cargo carrying all these supposed valuable rocks acquired the clearance with all speed and minimal fuss by the authorities?"

Old Wilkie hung his head, recalling the past. "Perhaps," he said gloomily, "but I was a wreck nursing a raging fever at the loss of my moon rock with many woeful terrible financial worries at the time and thought nothing of it."

"Assuredly so, as you were meant to," I said tactfully.

"But how did you ever . . .?"

I laid my hand compassionately on his shoulder as I answered, "Your reluctance to return to Morocco, which is just as well. Had you returned it would have been your death at the hands of thieving knaves rather than poor Altaf Gazra Ben-Chodo's, the merchant. He paid the price with his life I'm afraid."

"You mean . . . the murderous fiends?"

"Yes, my friend, the rocks that you have here are no ordinary carboniferous sills but contain jadeite in visible amounts. Just look at the emerald green. I suspect the hidden route into Morocco came out of China through Burma. I'm quite convinced that should we examine these rocks further you'll find me to be correct as to the jadeite and nephrite content concealed in each. Both extremely valuable commodities in the black market, and renowned for their rarity."

Surprise changed to incredulity in the moments it took for my host to fully grasp the significance of my revelations. He was speechless. I gently said, "Sir Wilkie, justice demands you contact the authorities in Morocco without delay to ensure that dastardly crimes such as this are prosecuted."

Sir Nigel shook his head helplessly at the enormity of the jewel-grade rocks that had lain in his possession all these years without his knowledge. His impatience to take the next step, to handle what must rightfully be done, to expose the crime to the rightful people was exceeded only by his urgency on the whereabouts of the moon rock.

"You're looking at it!" I replied simply.

Indeed he was. Of the eleven glass cases filling the Morocco Room one was left untouched. The rock within was of similar size as the rest, distinguished by its colour composition of a darkish grey silvery hue that closely resembled any carbonated iron ore substance, but was not of the earth. Old Wilkie gasped with a gaze so wondrous that he feared he could be mistaken, alternating between staring at his exhibit, then searching my face for tell-tale signs or clues that I had indeed grown mad or were playing a cruel joke. He could not take his gaze off the *moon.*

"Yes, Sir Wilkie, you've had your moon rock all along, safe under your roof."

"But the broken chest, the red fake blood stains, the locked room . . .?"

"It was never placed in the Moroccan chest. The trickery and flakiness of thieves in joint venture know no bounds! You have Ben-Chodo to thank. His gamble paid off!"

Sir Wilkie agreed, delighted by the turn of events "Moon to earth, moonbeams to earth-shimmer, mystery to magic, I think it all goes to prove that the *Bizarre* resides in the *Real*. Now Gigi leave me alone for a bit, will you? Let me gloat," he said with a wink, chuckling quietly, hugging his glass case, studying the moon rock with a look so desperate I feared he would never stop gazing.

"Where's the champagne?" I wanted to know.

"On ice."

"How long will you be?"

"A moment. Fetch the bottle."

The mystery of the Morocco room having been solved; I spent a restful three weeks in sunny Penang before taking myself off to Bali en route to my hometown of Oswego, while Sir Wilkie Tang attended to business. I must confess the rest of my vacation was pleasant befitting an American holiday-maker pursuing an idyllic chapter in one's life than unearthing treacherous buried tales, robbery and murder or locked room mysteries, however cozy or tempting.

Needless to say Old Wilkie accompanied me.

Rekha Valliappan

Rekha Valliappan is a multi-genre writer of various short stories published in dozens of international magazines and journals. They include a range of weird fiction, literary, mystery & suspense, and dark fiction. She has won awards for her writing and earned nominations for the Pushcart Prize and Best of the Net. Of the many among others she is the author of 'The Compass Turns Thrice' which appeared in Litro Magazine, 'Elephant Sutra' published in New World Writing, and more recently 'The Mirror Effect' in Penumbric Speculative Fiction Magazine. A full list of all her works appear on her website silicasun.wordpress.com She also writes poetry and has seen her poems featured in Press 53/Prime Number Magazine, Nixes Mate Review, Madras Courier, and elsewhere

Caravaggio Absconded Dweller in Tenebrism

Jasiah Witkofsky

A manmade rasp replicating the hoot of the ghost owl alerted the rider in black of the score. Drawing a mask completely over his head, he kicked his horse into action. Charging down the moonlit road, he reined in his mount when the light of a swaying lantern from an approaching coach became visible.

Turning the stallion off the well-driven path, the dark-clad figure waited amidst the pines and underbrush. When the wheels of the transport became audible, the horseman trotted forward and aimed his matchlock straight at the driver.

"Discard your arquebus and blades…then step down and tell those within to exit, leaving their weapons inside. I have musketeers behind you and more men in the woods so do not attempt any acts of bravery and you shall remain unharmed."

The startled wagoner complied to the rogue's request, dropping his armaments and calling down the man inside through a slot in the cabin. The protector of the delivery exited the wagon to be greeted by a man garbed in a duster pointing a rifle at his chest, fuse at the ready.

The highwayman ordered the two teamsters to lay flat beneath the carriage as the horseman set the mules drawing the cart free, scattering them into the night. The rifleman found the mark inside a protective slot beneath the cabin's roof. Drawing the large package from the wagon, he signalled to his comrade and made off into the darkness.

The horseman kept his gun trained on the hostages, pathetically prone upon the dusty road. When he felt his partner had been given enough of a lead to escape with their treasure. He fired a celebratory shot into the air and raced off after his companion.

▼▼▼

"I am most pleased you have arrived so promptly, Madame Llorenc." Fra Matteo placed his palms upon the desk, his desperation palpable. "The situation is most dire and needs to be handled with stealth and alacrity… this is why I have called upon you."

The woman addressed by the broker, bloused in white, contrasting sharply with the dark, tight pantaloons and boots of a horseman, tossed and caught her dagger absently as she spoke.

"Continue…"

The mahogany curls beneath the ex-monk's tight cap trembled as he wiped sweat from his brow and straightened his posture to look directly into the golden-brown eyes of the beautiful Catalonian adventurer. Somehow, her apparent innocence and carefree demeanour was just as bold and intimidating as any steel-gazed mercenary Matteo had employed. A brave warrior knew fear, but this petite and effeminate figure was neither imbecilic nor cognizant of terror. It was one thing to know fright, another altogether to brush it aside as if the emotion was nothing more than a gnat.

Fra Matteo weighed his options then made his choice. "I have no other alternative but to come to the quick of it then. Before the passing of the late, great Michelangelo Merisi da Caravaggio, artist, duellist, outlaw…a character I'm sure you would have fancied. But I deviate, before Caravaggio's death, the papacy commissioned him to paint a rendition of the Virgin Mary with the new-born Christ."

Fra Matteo took this opportunity to unravel a scroll from amongst his innumerable papers, revealing the imagery to Dolores. The hyperrealism of the charcoal sketch forced Dolores's eyes to widen like a doe and purse her lips, nearly salivating at the exquisite perfection of the curvature and shading imprinted upon the quality pulp. Although the babe was supposed to be the focal point of the draft, the reclining form of the Mother of God evoked a living voluptuousness that seemed impossible to reproduce upon a flat surface…illusory magic at its finest. Dolores caught her break in composure and quickly handed the masterpiece back to her employer as she reclaimed her poise.

"You make an overabundant emphasis towards minutia, Matteo, so explain to me what is pertinent? What are you hinting at with all of this meandering about?"

Gulping, Matteo carefully retired the drawing and continued, "This is an original from the master himself. I should know, I was there with my benefactor when he made the initial transaction. What you have just perceived is the first draft of what the mad genius began, but never finished, putting on canvas. I bore witness to this incomplete work, and though the piece was never finalized, the inception was so noteworthy that my client spent a small fortune procuring it. I have the bill of receipt here." He produced the formally signed documents that proved ownership of the purchase.

"Somewhere along the route of delivery, between here and Varese, the artwork was stolen by a band of highwaymen during the night. Upon the morn we learned of this robbery and immediately sent men out the main roads for investigation and made the call out to you. My benefactor allowed me to borrow this sketch so I could show you some idea of what the unfinished product looks like. I know you have a sharp eye for detail and since I have seen the canvas, allow me to describe it to you further.

"The width is nearly the length of your arm-span, and the height is approximately the distance from the ground to your navel. The edges that surround the central focal point are as black as can be, like much of Caravaggio's works, for he took Da Vinci's chiaroscuro techniques and amplified it tenfold. The colorations of the figures remain incomplete, and the underlying charcoal is still visible. Regardless, it is a breath-taking piece of incomparable craftsmanship."

Dolores waved on the wordy intellectual, "Get to the point Matteo, you said time was of the essence, so spare me the prattle and please inform me why I was made to rush to your office."

Matteo rubbed the tension from his temples and continued, "Apologies, you are correct to be impatient. Allow me to impart some more vital bits of information. There was a heavy bidding war for this artwork with the wealthy merchant-prince, Niccolò Conti of La Spezia, not far from here fortunately. Only a handful of people would have been aware of this shipment, which was specifically targeted. *Signore* Conti appears to be the most likely suspect behind this theft.

"I am responsible for the recovery of my employer's property, and you and your cohorts are the most capable to fulfil such an endeavour. Large amounts of finances were spent in the procurement of this one-of-a-kind commodity, thus I sought out the services of the best. To assuage your concerns, I have been allotted a generous sum to pay for your services."

A sizeable purse of silver was deposited upon the desk. Dolores estimated there was enough there to live extravagantly for years. Feigning nonchalance, she decided to strike a higher bargain.

"This expedition will require some number of resources. I shall need all the accoutrements necessary to infiltrate high society. And though the offer is generous, I feel my deeds require a compensation befitting the pursual of such an endeavour. I will enlist my regiment to undertake said mission, for this payment…in addition to that sketch you just displayed. I feel that is both fair and fitting."

The broker clutched the scroll protectively, "It is not within my power to offer this as part of the deal, it remains the property of my employer. When his painting is safely returned to him, then I will ask if he will be willing to part with this art piece."

Dolores picked up her riding cape and throwing it over her shoulder, said, "No need Fra Matteo…I will ask him myself. Besides, I need to speak directly to him."

"But…but…Madame, that is completely unseemly." Matteo stammered, "My client is a very busy man."

"He'll make time if he wants his precious painting back." She flashed her bright smile, "I have a plan I will describe to you on the road. Besides…you talk too much to be a middleman."

▼▼▼

The travel down the coast to La Spezia was swift and uneventful. Dolores rented a carriage and had her men drive her to the Conti villa overlooking the Tyrrhenian Sea.

It turned out *Signore* Alessandro Peroraro was indeed a very busy man. So enmeshed in his letters and ledgers, Dolores found it refreshingly easy to finagle the financier to acquiesce to her requests, his terse agreements utilized to remove her distractions from pressing affairs. She smoothed the ruffles of the gaudy, voluminous dress she procured from his daughter's wardrobe, quickly hemmed to adjust the material to her petite size. The heavy signet ring of the Peroraro house had to be slipped over a thin band of silver to fit upon her middle finger, another borrowed prop for her disguise.

Dolores Llorenc now played the role of Madame Katrina Luiz Montenegro, the half-Castilian mistress of *Signore* Peroraro. The missive had been sent and the return invitation delivered. So, she made the jostling route, curled hair pinned high, and face painted in the current fashion of the elites.

Her entourage, garbed in the uniforms of the Peroraro offices, parked before the manor house and ushered the lady incognito to the entryway, two of whom remained ever-present at her side.

"*Signora* Montenegro." The man of the house introduced himself to Dolores with grace, respect, and a hint of undeniable lust in the corners of his eyes, the man welcomed his guest into his household.

He stopped throughout the entry and main hall to show off his collection of busts and portraits he had amassed throughout his life, a story behind each piece. Finally, they attained the study where two men sat in heated conversation. Offering her a glass of his latest vintage and a seat, he formally introduced the newcomer to his guests.

"Lady Katrina Montenegro, may I grace your presence to two of my foreign associates. The esteemed Comandante Pierre Laurent of Toulouse and my long-time friend, Gustav Xenakis hailing from Macedonia."

Pleasantries were received and dishes of olives and cold-pressed meats from the estate's groves were passed around before Dolores engaged the nucleus of her undertaking.

"*Signore* Conti, I do not wish to appear rude in front of your guests from afar, and to you in your own domicile. But I was hopeful to attain a private meeting regarding my primary purpose for intruding upon your schedule."

Niccolò set his glass down to address the lady, "Madame, whatever need be said can be proclaimed before all present. The Comandante is a man of honour and Gus I have known since childhood. So, feel free to speak your piece, I have naught to hide in front of these two."

Dolores shifted in her seat as all eyes fixated upon her, "I come here today at the behest of the Peroraro company to retrieve property that has been hijacked enroute to the owner's estates within Genoa. My master has sent me in his stead to rectify what appears to be an injustice of note towards my benefactor. As the message sent to you dictated, we wished to settle this matter without publicity or interference of the authorities to maintain friendly relations between our two firms. Nonetheless, as far as we know the purchase was unknown to everyone save *Signore* Peroraro, the seller of said artifact, and yourself, if I may be so blunt?"

Niccolò Conti rubbed his chin, looking both perplexed and mildly affronted. "Yes, I am aware of the travesty of this situation. Tis true, I competed with *Signore* Peroraro for the Caravaggio, but I freely concede that

I was not willing to part with the sums he was offering to pay. I may have been in opposition with Alessandro on this particular issue, but I have always dealt fairly in mercantile situations."

The conversation was interrupted by the entrance of a woman bedecked in spring green led by an effeminate young man in a beret and followed by a maiden dressed more extravagantly than the aristocratic fringe and military pomp of the other denizens who lounged decadently within the study. Niccolò Conti gestured them within in familiarity and introduced the new arrivals.

"Please, allow me to acquaint you to my lovely wife, Isabella, my beautiful daughter Magdalena, and my second son, Otto, an artist in apprenticeship who I am most proud of. One of his works is displayed over the mantle."

The room stood to gawk at the oil depiction of Augustus Octavius Caesar before the Colosseum of Rome as Dolores gazed at the matron of the house. Beautiful despite her advanced years and somehow so familiar. When the audience finished complimenting the shy artist, Dolores reinjected herself into the menagerie.

"I do not wish to take away from your son's fine accomplishment, but business takes precedent over pleasure as the wise often say. If we can resume the discussion at hand, then the swifter I can allow you all to continue your pleasantries…may I be so bold?"

"Forgive me *Senorita*…Madame. I meant no affront or diversion. Paternal pride often gets the best of me, but back to the topic at hand, as you say. Magdalena, my dear…can you please summon the rest of the household?

I wish to assure our guest that we do not possess the artifact so she can more quickly find the true culprit of this heinous crime."

"Papa! Must I? Even Lorenzo?" The landlord's daughter pouted.

"Of course! Do as I say, *ragazza*! Gather all your siblings, I am here to show the Lady Montenegro that my family acts in the best of faith and that we have naught to hide." The maiden's father rolled his eyes and threw his arms into the air in an exaggerated gesture at his daughter's pettiness.

Turning on her heels, the young Magdalena stormed out of the study with her nose in the air.

"Forgive my daughter, she is youthful and brash, but I will not altogether deny her her defiant spirit, a Conti trait that will keep her from being trounced upon." Niccolò offered his wife and son a drink and topped off everyone else's glass. "While we wait for my summons, is there any questions you wish to ask of me Lady Montenegro?"

Dolores swirled the wine in her hand, looking down at the clear magenta liquid. "As I said, I was informed that it was just you and my Alessandro who bid over the Caravaggio…is that true?"

"Others may have known that the piece was up for sale, I am not sure of this, but yes, only myself and *Signore* Peroraro made any direct offers…that is true. We may have been the only ones who could have afforded such a rarity." The patriarch shrugged and looked her full in the face.

She pressed further, "And what made you wager so

high? From what I was told, it was quite the competition between you two."

The host chuckled, "Yes, your sponsor and I played a gruelling game of high stakes. But, at the risk of repeating myself, I run my interactions with the utmost of honour and fairness. I realized Alessandro was willing to sacrifice more for the exchange. I would never lower myself to steal a lost purchase like a lowly highwayman.

"As for my love of high art, this has been my greatest passion as far back as I can recall. My largest vice is my obsession to further my vast collection, as you can well see, *Senorita* Montenegro."

"It is very true, Lady Katrina." The Greek chimed in, "As wee lads, he had my father bring him to Athens to see the sights. Any chance to view a new piece and he will be the first through the doorway."

It was at this point that a highly perturbed Magdalena returned with the addition of two young men, hair the same honey-brown colour as her own. One, moustachioed and in the military regalia of the principality and the other, younger one in a fine evening jacket of crimson and gold. Niccolò rushed between the two excitedly.

"And here are the final members of my household. Lady Katrina Montenegro, I would like you to meet my eldest, *Signore* Amadeo, home for leave, and my youngest, Lorenzo."

Now that Dolores had everyone gathered, she let them settle before proceeding on with the investigation. "If I can draw your attention towards me, I would like to get to the heart of the matter."

She pulled a rolled paper from a large purse and unraveled the scroll. "I am curious if anyone has seen the painting based on this sketch?" She slowly walked the image around the room, noting the awe of the onlookers. She registered the tense shiftiness in the gaze of one individual into her mental reservoirs.

As Dolores received negatory responses from all save Niccolò, she caught the blush upon his wife and suddenly made the connection. Without thinking, she blurted out, pointing. "You are the woman drawn! You posed as the Virgin Mary for Caravaggio!"

Isabella's blush deepened as gasps broke out amongst the hoity-toity, with all eyes turning between the sketch and the matriarch. Composing herself, Isabella attempted to regain her poise in the situation.

"Yes, Lady Katrina, I was the model for this project. I was not much younger than you, my daughter." She averted her eyes to Magdalena, imploring forgiveness with her pleading gaze. "It is true, Michelangelo managed to convince me to disrobe for his portrayal. At the time, I felt quite honoured to be chosen by the artist that many deemed the greatest of his era…it was before I met your father. I assure you all, it was quite the innocent undertaking, and I did not bed *Signore* Caravaggio. Still, I see not what this has to do with *Senorita* Montenegro's inquiries?"

Dolores cocked an eyebrow, "Quite the coincidence, would you not agree?"

Niccolò stepped forward in a protective gesture, "Lady Katrina, up to now I did obfuscate this one detail, I did not wish to embarrass my beautiful wife. But yes, this was a large part of why I desired this painting so much. The most noteworthy artist depicting the most beautiful woman I have ever met…this pierces the heart of my desires for this particular work."

Isabella tugged upon her husband's sleeve, "And why could you not retrieve this holy depiction for me? You let some other man hold possession of my visage?"

"My dear, calm yourself." Niccolò replied defensively, "I did all within my power to secure this piece. I could not match the finances of *Signore* Peroraro. His Genoese ties to the sea outstrip my own humble portside connections, I sorely admit."

Dolores decided to interrupt this lover's spat for the sake of all present. "The abduction of this fine work happened precisely five nights previous, do all of you have assurances of your whereabouts upon that evening?"

The French commander and Amadeo the soldier relayed that they were on route from their military posts as Isabella and Otto were at home, applying lace and refining skills at brushwork, respectively. Gustav the Greek met his lifetime friend, Niccolò, upon the road on the way back from the Papal states following his failed negotiations for the object in question. All eyes swivelled upon the two youngest siblings of the Conti family. The Comandante Pierre took this opportunity to step forward by Dolores's side.

"*Mademoiselle*, it seems as though you have narrowed down your options, but are you certain that the perpetrator of this heinous offense walks amongst us?"

Magdalena interjected in her defence, "I was adjourning the town that evening with my friends. Any of them would vouch for my whereabouts upon that night…which were innocent I assure you."

Dolores directed her attention at the youngest of the Conti family, "And you Lorenzo, where were you upon that pivotal Friday evening?"

The young man shifted his glances throughout the gathering, then turned his head to stare at his feet. "I was sent to follow my sister…to make sure she was not up to any unseemly behavior."

"You pervert!" Screamed Magdalena, "Who would dare send this beast to spy upon me?"

Isabella confronted her daughter, "It was I who ordered Lorenzo to follow you, my lovely. I wished for you to remain safe and not fall under the temptations of sin and the evils of the city."

"As you would have done, you whore!" Magdalena yelled at the top of her lungs, "You don't want me to end up like you, the slut that you are? And you send this vile slime to follow me, the very one who raped my dear friend, Dahlia and tried to take advantage of me!"

"Enough!" Niccolò roared, trying to regain some control over his household. "I will have no more of these wild accusations. We are a family, and we shall act as such…"

A rap at the door was answered by one of Dolores's attendants. He returned to whisper into her ear as Niccolò attempted to smooth over the drama that erupted amongst his loved ones. She cleared her throat loudly to interrupt the awkward situation.

"It has come to my attention that a stallion within your stables matches the description of the steed used in the robbery of my master's acquisition. We have one of the survivors of the crime here with us as witness to this claim."

"Everyone! To your feet." *Signore* Conti ordered, "We shall settle this matter once and for all. I shall have no more dishonour upon my name."

Niccolò Conti led the march to the barn as the setting sun cast long shadows about the well-manicured property. The fenced field that caged the grazing equestrians was attended by stable hands feeding and brushing down the majestic steeds that dotted the landscape. All the work staff stood at attention when their master neared.

Dolores signalled her men to bring the coachman over, "This was the driver who made the highjacked delivery. Did you have something you would like to say?"

The man pointed out the horse that bore one of the men that robbed their carriage. "The stallion yonder, I clearly remember those three beige spots on the rear."

Niccolò looked startled now that direct evidence was found on his estate. He questioned the man with a frantic urgency, "Did you get a look at the robber…any signifying features…his face?"

"No *Signore*." The coachman stammered, "He wore all black and his face was completely covered."

Niccolò began to pace frantically, tugging agitatedly at his clothes. "Boy! Where is Alphonse? I want my driver here, now!"

"I…I don't know." A stableboy answered meekly, "I haven't seen him in some time."

"Scour the yard! Sweep the barn! I want him found immediately." Niccolò fumed and ranted at all who toiled beneath him.

Dolores took this opportunity to slide over to Magdalena and whisper a private conversation with the young woman, during which the estate burst into a frenzy of activity. When it appeared that Niccolò had regained some control over his rational faculties, Dolores returned to the crux of the matter.

"One question does come to my mind. Lorenzo, you said you followed your sister on the night of question, can you tell me what establishments she frequented that evening?"

The young lad looked taken aback, "Uhhh…*L'Acino Acido*, I have people to verify this."

"You lying snake!" Magdalena screeched, "I would never frequent one of your seedy taverns. I was viewing a rendition of the lost tales of Prometheus. For every friend you were able to bribe to retell your falsehood, I will provide ten witnesses to prove my attendance."

The spat between the youngest siblings was interrupted by a shout from the barn. The party hastened their way towards the commotion as two servants walked a large object down from the loft. Unveiling the flat object, the gathering stood frozen in awe as the missing Caravaggio was revealed before all.

"We found this behind the haybales." One of the handlers explained.

Niccolò recovered from his shock and addressed everyone in an authoritative tone. "How did this get stashed upon my residence unbeknownst to me? This implicates all of us in a very serious offense. I know some here can vouch for their whereabouts with veracity, but there must be a guilty party responsible for this theft. I demand answers, immediately!"

Dolores drew the conversation away from entering another tangent, "The discrepancy between Magdalena's and Lorenzo's stories has not been fully addressed. I find this both intriguing and disturbing."

The Comandante nodded in support of Dolores's implication as Magdalena rushed forward to her father to clutch his hand. "Papa! You must believe me! I would never do anything so dreadful as this. Every word I spoke is the truth."

"I find it hard to believe that a frail, young girl could pull off such a daring manoeuvre, no matter who may have been assisting her." Chimed the Frenchman as all eyes turned on Lorenzo. The youngest member of the Conti family could no longer hold his composure as sweat beaded heavy upon his suddenly colourless face, and a quaking of the hands that he could no longer control.

"Son." The senior Conti engaged his progeny with smooth and even tones. "Do you have something to tell me. I love you as dearly as anyone, and if you have anything to say, I am the one who shall best understand your situation."

The tender note in his father's voice broke the young man who fell to his knees, bawling at Niccolò's feet. "Papa, I'm so sorry. I was bribed into this. A man in the night waylaid me and offered silver to steal a painting if I were to give it to you. I was waiting for your birthday to show you. It seemed like an opportunity to good to be true…so I succumbed, paid Alphonse to assist me, and we made the ride to procure your gift…please father!

No one was harmed. I did this for you."

Niccolò shook his head slowly in shame before slapping his son full force in the face, knocking him into the dust of the road.

"You have disgraced the family and my business, possibly beyond repair. Tie this degenerate to the horse fence."

Manservants rushed forward to fulfil their lord's request as Niccolò grabbed a horsewhip. When his son was roped firmly to the posts, Niccolò Conti began lashing the youth with a fury that shocked the onlookers. Lorenzo's wails drowned out the weeping of his mother when Dolores stepped forward to stop the brutal flogging.

"I do not wish to interfere with how you conduct business or deal with your family, but I believe that all accounts have been settled if the depiction of our Holy Mother is delivered safely back to *Signore* Peroraro."

Drawing deep breaths of air, Niccolò managed to calm himself. He had his servants carefully bundle the Caravaggio after one last wistful look and placed safely within the Lady's carriage as Lorenzo was untied from the fencing, falling unconscious upon the road.

With her investigations concluded, Dolores directed her men to prepare for the return to La Spezia. As she mounted the transport, *Signore* Conti came bearing a package which he unwrapped, revealing a small bust cast in bronze. He handed the sculpture over to Dolores.

"Lady Katrina Luiz Montenegro, I would appreciate it most sincerely if you were to deliver this to your master. Modelled from the Duchess Margherita de 'Medici by my son's teacher, the Maestro Biscaino. I give this in the desire to maintain cordial relations between our two houses…even after the shame my youngest has now stained our name with. I should have sent him off to the clergy, but alas, I let him sit idle at home. I hope to send this off with you in the spirit of renewal between the Conti and Peroraro."

Dolores accepted the offering and closed the meeting with as much tact as she could muster. "This is a most generous and gracious gesture, *Signore* Conti. Let me divulge that I need not report all details to my benefactor, in fact, I might just spin things as if Alphonse was the primary culprit of this botched forfeiture."

Niccolò Conti beamed a smile of great relief, kissed the Lady's hand, and shut the carriage door for her. He stood in the fading light, waving his farewells as the small company from Genoa departed the manicured estates and made way to the city that caressed the coastline.

▼▼▼

Dolores Llorenc departed the offices of Fra Matteo with payment for services rendered swiftly and beyond expectations. She made her way to *La Tettarella del Drago*, the favourite establishment of the Crimson Cinquedeas gang, where the constabulary was paid off to stay well enough away. She found her friend, Jerome the Moor, who divvied out sizeable amounts to all members involved before they departed in separate directions to celebrate their success.

Dolores received a glass of wine and sat across from her friend, "We just pulled off the most elaborate double-cross of all double-crosses, with none the wiser and no harm done, except for the poor lad who took some punishment as scapegoat for our caper."

Jerome scoffed, "Bah...He was a bully and a rapist. His punishment could have been far more severe. Exile...death...castration even."

Dolores winced at her friend's harsh proclamation, but continued, "He received some retribution for his crimes, I witnessed it personally. And thanks to our forethought and spies in all the right places, we were able to root out his sins and utilize them to our own advantage."

"Didn't hurt to have a mole in your Fra's library as well. It was far too easy to threaten that spoiled whelp into conceding to our requests. He fell into the ploy like a rat lured by cheese to the trap." Jerome quaffed a good quantity of ale, foam lingering on his beard.

"True enough. Still, I can't help but feel some small remorse for our deeds...although, I did so enjoy watching those aristocratic snobs sweat." She sipped from her glass gingerly.

"Ha ha, *ragazza.* I wish I could have seen all that transpired. But my ugly face has no business mucking with nobility." Jerome laughed. "But your plan was ingenious...staging the heist that you knew you would get hired to solve. Now that is a fine work of art, my Madame Pistollera." He raised his tankard in a ruffian's salute.

Dolores tore a chunk of bread from her friend's loaf and changed the course of the conversation. "You mentioned something earlier Jerome...is it true you knew

Caravaggio?"

The rogue glanced whimsically at the roof as he recalled years previous, "Aye *ragazza*, I was much younger then. Back when I was apprenticing and assisting with colouring church murals. Merisi was quite the bandit…he would have worn the crimson well. But by the divinities, he could fight. A man better to have on your side than against."

Dolores carefully produced a scroll from her satchel and slid it over to her long-time companion. "I almost gifted this to the Lady Conti since she was the subject matter for the piece…but I decided that you should have something from a friend now departed."

Jerome unraveled the scroll and his mouth dropped. Moisture misted over his dark eyes as he turned his attention back upon his friend. "*Ragazza*…beautiful…"

He dropped the sketch and picked up the tiny woman from across the table to spin her about in his arms. "This is by leagues the greatest present I have ever received. You honour me beyond my worth, Madame."

He yelled amidst the bustle of the inn's lively atmosphere, "Everyone, everyone! Until the midnight hour arrives, all drinks are paid, courtesy of me, Jerome. Strike a song, Leone."

The denizens of the establishment roared joyously as the lute was strummed into tune. Jerome continued to whirl his wee compadre about in his clumsy, heavy-booted manner as Dolores's laughter rang high and sweet into the night.

Jasiah Witkofsky

The antivillain known as Jasiah Witkofsky is an independent author, editor, philosopher-gardener, artistic dabbler, rock n' roller, and rabblerouser dwelling amidst the majestic Sierra Nevadas of Northern California. His works can be found on both hemispheres of the globe, three continents, from several anthology companies.

Find him under http://www.facebook.com/jasiahwitkofskyauthorpage

More From Nordic Press

Novels/Novellas

Face of Fear by C. Marry Hultman

9789198671001

Dawson Junior G3 by Brian Wagstaff

9789198671049

Boy in the Wardrobe by Esther Jacoby

9789198684018

New Life Cottage by Esther Jacoby

9789198671056

The Wait by Esther Jacoby

e-book:https://books2read.com/u/4Dgz8Q

Liebe ist Warten by Esther Jacoby

9789198671070

Das Cottage by Ester Jacoby

978919868407

Musing on Death & Dying by Esther Jacoby

9789198671063

Earth Door by Cye Thomas

9789198671025

An Odd Collection of Tales By Cye Thomes

9789198684124

Graffiti Stories by Nick Gerrard

9789198671018

Punk Novelette by Nick Gerrard

9789198671087

Struggle and Strife by Nick Gerrard

9789198684049

Fake Escape by Natalie Hughes

e-book:https://books2read.com/u/bMXL5X

Hell Hath No Fury by Chisto Healy

9789198750706

True Mates by E.F. Vogel

9789198750713

CHRONICLES

Six Days to Hell by E.L. Giles

9789198684087

Cold as Hell by Neen Cohen

9789198684094

Murder Planet by Adam Carpenter

9789198671032

Generation Ship by Adam Carpenter

9789198684063

Sunshine by L.T. Emery

978-9198750942

MYTHOS

Antisocial Housing by Tim Mendees

978-9198750959

ANTHOLOGIES

Just 13

9789198684025

Lost Lore & Legends

9789198671094

Rise and Fall

9789198750911

Worlds Collide

9789198750928

Wicked West
9789198684193

THE MORTEM CYCLE

Death House
978-9198684117

Death Ship
978-9198684148

Death Beyond
978-9198684162

Death Cuisine
978-9198684186

Death Magic
978-9198750904

Find us at:
http://www.nordicpresspublishing.com